My Mind Wonders

A book of short stories by Wendy Lawson

The Ha Ha Herman Publishing Company

Waskom, Texas

**This book is dedicated to Bettie and Clyde Lawson.
You are missed more than words can say.**

I have always been a daydreamer and a storyteller. I owe so much to my sisters and family for being so supportive of my flights of fancies.

Special thanks to my sister Rebecca Pilkington a.k.a. Proofreader, advisor, and sometimes unlicensed psychologist.

Life in a Bottle

"Lookie, the whole crazy gangs here."

Bob climbed out of the box that he now called home. He was mumbling to himself about the night before. "Don't know why you had to hit me in da head. I would have given you a drink. But, no you have to take my two dollas and fifty cent too." Bob rubs his head where he has a cut and a good size bruise. His head feels foggy as it does every morning. He kicks the box next to his and yells, "Hey, Crab git up, let's go get somethin to eat and I need a nip." The box shook some like Crab was moving around inside. His head pops out then. He has dirty blond hair that is all matted and a beard and mustache. One of his eyes wonders as he says, "You git up, you want everybody to git up. Here." He hands Bob a wine bottle with a couple of drinks in it and ducks back in. Bob drinks it down and throws the bottle into his own box for keeping. He grabs his backpack and puts it on his back. Bob knows from experience that you take anything that you want to keep with you. Crab crawls out of his box and pulls himself up using the wall of the building they have been sleeping beside. He has his pack in his hand and once he's standing he puts it on. Crab has a bad leg that causes him to walk with a sideways limp. That's where he got the nickname Crab. He looks over at Bob with his one eye wondering and says "Ok, you ole nag let's go." They hobble out of the alley and head to the catholic mission where they can eat breakfast. Crab asks, "What happen to yo head?" Bob tells him, "That goon Rex decided he wanted what I have. So he took it." Bob sees a can in the gutter and goes over and picks it up. He reaches behind him to a pocket on the side of his backpack and pulls out a plastic grocery bag and put the can in it. He sees a few more cans on the way and he looks in the trash cans and dumpsters where he finds some too. He has to beat the others to them. They run into Maggie on the way. She's pushing her baby stroller with her stuff in it. She has a bag with a few cans in it tied to the handle. They tell her good morning and she just "Humphs" and they walk the rest of the way to the mission.

When they arrive at the mission they get in line as usual. It isn't open yet but they know that if you don't get here early you might not get to eat. They stand in line listening to everybody talking, arguing, laughing and some are even sleeping. They finally open the door and everyone files in and makes their way down the buffet line. They are serving the usual eggs, sausage and biscuits, juice and coffee. They get their trays of food and find a table to sit at. Once seated Bob notices Rex standing in the buffet line. He whispers to Crab, "Look who's here, that stupid dope head Rex." Rex isn't paying any attention to him or Crab. Bob sees a dark spot the size of a bottle cap almost in the middle of his forehead. It's really dark like an ink spot or something. Rex gets his food and as he is walking to a table he falls out on the floor. He is lying on top of his food tray twitching and then he stops. The people in the mission all stop and stare. The mission workers who are serving the food come running out and one of them checks for a pulse and yells for another to call 911. He starts CPR and they wait for the ambulance to arrive. When they get there they put Rex on a stretcher and carry him out of the church. Everyone is quiet as they finish their breakfast.

After breakfast they sit through a sermon and then they go on their way. As they walk out Bob and Crab talk about Rex and wonder what happened. As they go along Bob notices spots on strangers that they pass. The spots vary in darkness from just foggy looking to ink black. Some people have more than one spot. They split ways to do their can and scrap collection for the days booze without Bob mentioning what he is seeing. He is getting the shakes and all he can think about is getting something to drink. Bob is going along his usual route collecting cans. He's finding a lot today. On a Wednesday too. He usually does better on the weekend or Monday. He's looking in a dumpster behind a convenience store when he sees a friend of his they call Rowdy. He notices a jar lid size dark spot over Rowdy's chest. Bob is speechless for a minute but Rowdy is shouting in his usual way, "Hey there, ole bud, how's it hanging?" He comes up on Bob and hits him on the back almost knocking him down. "What happened to your head? You been brawlin?" Bob is finally able to talk and he says, "Some duffus decided to part me from my money." Rowdy says, "Let's go get him. We'll get your money back." Bob says, "Rowdy, we can't. They took him to the hospital. He fell out earlier at the mission." Rowdy says, "Karma, my bud, karma." Bob can't help but look at Rowdy's chest. It's not quiet ink black, but it's dark. Rowdy says, "I know you didn't get your morning bottle so here take a good swig of mine." He hands Bob his paper bag wrapped bottle of wine. Bob drinks hungrily and hands it back. "I thought you were going to knock it out there a minute. I did pretty good yesterday; I found some copper pipe out at the dump. I had to sneak in." Bob is starting to feel better again. He is still missing his morning bottle though.

By eleven Bob had gathered enough cans to cash in and buy a bottle of wine. He was pretty shaky by then and the store clerk let him slide for a quarter. As soon as he had made it outside the store he went around back and drank half of it. He had been seeing the spots all morning. The store clerk even had a shadow on his front lower center. About where the pancreas is he thought. Bob used to be Dr. Robert Deville, a reputable family practice doctor until his whole life changed. He had left his home town of New Orleans, Louisiana to go to medical school and do his residency in Shreveport, Louisiana. That is where he met his wife Jill. She was working on becoming a registered nurse. They dated as much as they could with both of their schedules but Bob still fell hard. She was gorgeous. When they had been dating for about a year Jill got pregnant. She decided to have the baby being from a catholic family and Bob ask her to marry him knowing that it would be hard with both of them still in school. Her family didn't like him, knocking their daughter up and all. But everyone adjusted. The pregnancy was going fine until she was in her eighth month and went to a doctor's appointment. They couldn't hear a heartbeat. She had noticed that she wasn't feeling the movement that she had before and she was in pain. It was abruptio placentae, a complete separation between the baby and the placenta. The baby girl had died. Jill wasn't the same after that. She became angry and mean to Bob. She blamed him because she felt that he should have known. She even went so far as to say so in one of her many hysterical rants. He just kept thinking that it would pass. He went on to become a doctor and was offered a position at a reputable hospital in Nashville, Tennessee. He took it and him and Jill moved there. It wasn't long before he was invited to join a couple of doctors at a nice private practice clinic. With Jill still angry and mean, he started drinking to settle his nerves. That's what he told himself anyway. One morning while at the clinic with a severe hangover" he had taken a little nip to lighten it some" he gave a young kid with a pretty severe upper respiratory infection a dose of penicillin even though on his chart it said severely allergic. He went into anaphylactic shock and died. The partners already knew that he was having problems with his drinking. They asked for his resignation. He was sued and Jill left him almost before he could get the story told. He hit the booze hard and before he knew it he was living on the street. His family stopped talking to him. Now he is a homeless drunk.

Bob starts his can rounds. He has a path that he takes every day. Like gangs, homeless people have their own territories and they know where they can search. He finds an old aluminum wheel and that makes him very happy. He finishes his rounds and takes the wheel and the cans he has already collected to the scrap yard. He goes by the store and picks up three bottles of their cheapest wine. Then he makes his way down to the river where the bridge is. He has some friends that hang out there. A lot of homeless people camp there. There are burn barrels and campfires. He sees his friends, there's Rowdy, Maggie, J.J., Tom, and Crab. They all have a paper bag covered bottle of wine and they are drinking and talking. He looks around at them and sees that all of them have the spots. Rowdy's spot on his chest is the darkest. The others all have shadows on their right sides about where their livers would be, but there are also spots on other areas of their bodies too. Most just shadows. Bob thinks "Why do I keep thinking in body parts?" He says, "Lookie, the whole crazy gangs here."

They all laugh and Crab says, "And you fit right in." Bob asks, "Has anybody heard anything about Rex?" The guy they call Tom, he always wears camo, was in the Iraq war says, "I heard that he was DOA. That's what that pick pocket kid said. You know the one that hangs out at the bus stops. He was right at the door when they were putting him in the ambulance." Bob just said, "Oh." They hang out for a while and then they go to the mission for their evening meal. They get there early but there is still a long line. They barely get in. Bob knows when he sees this that they are serving fried catfish or something else really good. They must have gotten a supply from somewhere. Sometimes people donate food that they don't get often and somehow the word gets out. They go through the buffet line and find a place to sit. Bob is able to sit next to Crab. He looks around and there are a lot of spots in here. After the meal they get to listen to a sermon again. When the priest is done he tells them that their good friend Rex had passed and they say a prayer for him. Before they leave Bob goes up and talks to the priest Father O'Brian and ask just what was wrong with Rex. He tells him that Rex had a massive brain aneurism. He met back up with his friend Crab and they walk back to their alley. Lucky day, their boxes are still there. They sit with their backs against the wall of the building and they each pull out their evening bottle and talk about their day. Crab used to be a dock worker at a brewery before he was run over by a forklift. He started out on pain pills and became addicted and from there he started drinking. His leg was messed up pretty bad. Then he reinjured it in a motorcycle accident and after that they couldn't do much more with it. That is the reason for his unusual limp. It hurts him when he's sober so he tries not to be sober. Bob ask, "Did you notice the spot on Rexes forehead?" Crab answered, "I didn't notice any spot, what do you mean by a spot?" "Oh, I don't know, never mind." They drank their wine until they were ready to pass out and then crawled into their boxes and slept.

Bob awoke to the sound of yelling and as he crawls out of his box the pick pocket kid runs past with an old man chasing him. "You come back here you little bastard!" Bob sees a very dark jar lid size spot on the old man's chest as he is coming up the alley. All of a sudden the man grabs his chest, stops and falls to the ground. Crab has crawled out by this time and he is saying, "We need to find him some help." Bob says, "I'll go." He gets up and goes as quickly as he can out of the alley and to the store right next to it. He sticks his head into the store and says "A man fell down with his heart, call 911. He's in the alley." He turns around and heads back to where the old man is and kneels down and starts CPR. A younger man runs into the alley and sees Bob hovered over the old man and starts yelling, "What did you do to my Dad? Get off of him" and he grabs Bob by the back of his jacket and yanks him. Bob falls and rolls out of his reach. Crab yells, "He's helping the old man. He grabbed his chest like he was having a heart attack." Bob yells, "The store man is calling for help." The younger man stops then and kneels down and does CPR.

After all of the excitement Bob and Crab miss breakfast so they just make their usual routes and decide to meet at the mission for a sandwich at lunch. Bob finds his usual cans, just enough to get him another bottle at eleven. He is still seeing spots on everyone. When he gets to the mission, there's Crab standing and talking to Father O'Brian. Father O'Brian is the only one that doesn't have any spots. They are standing next to a card table with a big basket of sandwiches on it. Bob picks up a sandwich and opens it and starts eating it right away. Father O'Brian chuckles and says, "Are you hungry today my friend?" Bob looks embarrassed and says, "Oh, I'm sorry, I missed breakfast, I've been about ready to eat my own hand off." Father O'Brian says, "Well, I'm glad you made it here before that happened," and he chuckles again. Bob wipes his mouth on his sleeve and says, "Did Crab tell you about our morning?" "Yes, he did and I told him that I would have a talk with Christopher." He sees that Bob doesn't recognize who Christopher is and he says, "Pick pocket kid." Bob says, "Oh." "I better get going" and starts to leave." Father O'Brian reaches into the basket and takes a couple of sandwiches out and hands Bob and Crab each one. "Have a blessed day my friends." They both say, "Thanks, Father" and walk off in opposite directions.

Bob is walking along, he's already picked up one and a half grocery bags full of cans and he had found some copper wire to burn. He had put the wire in his backpack and was digging in a trash can at the little city park when he looks up and sees Rowdy. He can't help but stare because the spot on his chest has darkened a lot. He looks a little pale too. He says, "Hey, Rowdy how ya feelin? Rowdy who is always friendly says, "Not too good actually. Why are you taking my cans?" Bob says, "Rowdy, you know that this is my can. What's wrong with you?" He has his hand on his chest and his color turns gray. "Rowdy, I think something's wrong with you. You're holding your chest. Do you feel pain or pressure on your chest? Does your arm or neck hurt? At this point he just shakes his head yes. Bob takes him over to a bench and gets him to sit down. He says, "Rowdy, I need you to stay here. Just try to relax. I'm going to get you some help." Bob takes his backpack off and leaves it with Rowdy and runs as he hasn't run in a while. He goes in the first business that he sees. It's a bank and a security guard stops him. He tells the security guard that there is a man having a heart attack in the park. He says, "Could you please call an ambulance?" The guard sees how upset Bob is and says, "Sure, Sure, just calm down, I'll go call now. Where is he?" Bob tells him that he is across the street down the walk a little ways on a bench. The guard says, "You go back over and I'll go call." Bob says, "Ok, tell them to hurry" and runs back over to the park. When he gets back to the bench Rowdy is leaned back and he looks terrible. Bob sits beside him and holds his hand and tells him that help is on the way. "You just hang in there." It doesn't take long for the ambulance to get there and they take Rowdy away. When they are loading him Bob ask, "Where are you taking him?" They tell him which hospital and Bob decides he'll go over and check on him later after he got his booze money. After Bob is done finding his cans for the day he cashes them in and then goes to the hospital to check on Rowdy. When he gets there he goes to the emergency area to find out which room he's in. He doesn't know Rowdy's real name so he just ask them about bums that were brought in. They tell him that he has to be a relative. Bob tells them, "I'm his brother." They asks him why he doesn't know his real name then and he replies that he is the only one he's got. Rowdy is an only child and his parents are both gone. They agree to let Bob go up to see him. Rowdy is in the ICU. When he gets to his room he peeks in the door and there is Rowdy hooked up to all of the equipment. He isn't conscious. He steps into the room further and stands and looks at him. A nurse comes in and looks at Bob disgusted and he asks her what happened. She tells him that he will have to talk to the doctor. The nurse leaves and Bob walks over to the side of his bed and he doesn't know what to do. He reaches out and pats Rowdy's hand lying limply on the bed and says, "Get well ole bud" and turns around and leaves. When he gets back down on the street his throat hurts. He feels like crying. He really doesn't know Rowdy that well, truth be told. He looks around for a place to sneak a nip and sees a bush. He steps behind it and takes a good swig. The wine makes him feel a little better so he steps back out and heads toward the river.

When he gets to the river all of his friends are standing around the barrel. Almost all of them anyway. He tells them about Rowdy. They talk softly between themselves for a while and then split ways. Bob and Crab walked together back to their alley. That evening while they are sitting against the wall drinking their evening bottle he tells Crab about the spots. He tells him about how the spots seem to show up darker when something is about to happen. Crab just listens. He doesn't ask if he has any. Bob just figures that he doesn't want to know. The next day Bob did something different. When he went in to buy his eleven o'clock bottle he ask the clerk if he had been feeling shaky, dizzy or been urinating frequently. The clerk looked at him strangely and asks, "How did you know that? I haven't been feeling well in awhile." Bob said, "You may be a diabetic. You probably won't believe this but I used to be a doctor before I became a bum." That's all that he said. He just took his bottle and left the store. When he got outside he couldn't believe what he had done. He hadn't told anyone but Crab about his life as a doctor and he had made Crab promise not to tell anyone ever.

He goes about his day still seeing the spots. He looks at people closer than he ever has. Almost everyone he passes has at least one shadow. He hasn't seen a child with spots yet though. He is walking along when he comes to the park that he and Rowdy were in when he had his heart attack. He hears someone speaking into a microphone. It sounds like a politician. Bob mutters, "Liars, all liars." But he still walks into the park to where he sees a group of people. They are all holding signs and up on stage is a middle aged man wearing a white dress shirt and gray slacks. He has dark curly hair and there is a woman and a little girl standing beside him. The little girl looks to be about twelve years old or so and he would guess that they are the family of the man speaking. He can't help but notice the big dark spot on the little girl's forehead. The man has a shadow on his right side about where his liver would be and the woman has a shadow over her chest. He looks at the signs and reads, "Jack Johnson for Senate!" Everyone is really involved with what the man is saying. They are shaking their heads and yelling "Yeah!" and stuff. He is telling them how he is going to help the poor and homeless. Bob is thinking, "Yeah, right. Like that will happen." His attention is drawn back to the girl. The spot is really dark. It's not as dark as Rex's was, but it wouldn't be long before it is. Bob thinks, "The poor child, this can't be good." Bob stands to the side and after a while it looks like they are finishing up. He doesn't know what to do. They won't believe a bum. He makes his way through the crowd, most of them move out of his way. They act like they don't want him to touch them. When he reaches the front of the stage he eases to the right and follows the edge until he is to the side of the stage. No one notices what he is doing. He sneaks around the side to the back where he sees steps. He just waits there. It's surprising how people in the city get so used to homeless people that they don't even notice them. When Jack Johnson comes down the steps with his wife and daughter Bob grabs his sleeve and tells him loudly, "I need to talk to you. It's about your daughter." At the mention of his daughter he gets a scared look on his face and looks over at his body guards. Without another word the two very large men in suits come toward him and each one grabs an arm and they drag him over to the side. One of them gets up close to his face and tells him, "You will not approach Mr. Johnson or his family again. If we see you anywhere near any of them we will have you arrested or make you wish that we had you arrested. Whatever our mood is that day. Do you understand?" All that Bob can do is shake his head yes. His eyes are tearing up because he is truly worried about the little girl. When they let him go he starts yelling, "There is something wrong with her head. You need to take her to have a cat scan. Please, Please." Mr. Johnson is looking at him. The two body guards look like they are about to beat him up. Bob backs away. He turns around and runs. He doesn't go far before he finds a bench and plops down on it and takes his bottle out and takes a big swig. He is breathing hard. He says to himself, "What is wrong with you? You finally lost your whole mind." And he takes another big drink and puts his bottle back into his backpack. He sits there as the crowd breaks up. He finally stands and starts walking. He feels dazed but he still goes along looking through trash cans and in gutters for cans. He knows that he can't go without his wine. He keeps thinking about the little girl. That evening as he sits in his alley drinking his wine he talks to Crab about the little girl. Crab says he'll think about it too and maybe they will come up with some way to help.

The next morning he wakes up with Crab kicking his box for a change. Bob crawls out and Crab tells him, "I know what we can do. We can write down what you know and get the note to him somehow. Maybe we can put it under his door or I know we can get Christopher to put it in his pocket. He's good at getting in people's pockets. Bob is shaking off his morning fog. He laughs and says it might just work. "Come on we need to talk to Christopher." They grab their backpacks; take a couple of morning swigs and head off to the mission. When they get there, they get their breakfast and watch for him. When they spot him he is heading out of the door and they don't waste any time. Neither of them knows him very well, but they catch him outside the mission. He only looks to be fourteen or fifteen years old, but he has that raggedy homeless look and eyes that look older. Bob says, "Hey Kid, how's it going?" Christopher looks at them with suspicion and says, "I'm making it? Why?" Bob says, "I know we haven't exactly been introduced. I'm Bob and this is Crab." He says, "I've heard your names around. So, what's up?" Bob and Crab look at each other and Bob says, "I guess there is only one way to do this and it's just putting it out there. We need your help." Christopher asks, "What's in it for me?" Bob tells him "This is a good deed. It's all about karma; you do something good and good comes to you." Christopher says, "Oh man, are you pulling my leg? You must be kidding." Bob says, "We need to save a little girls life. Follow us into the Church to talk to Father O'Brian and you can hear how." The young being so curious and all, he follows.

 Crab asks, "What are we doing going back in here? Bob tells him, "I need to talk to Father O'Brian." They find Father O'Brian kneeling before a statue of Mother Mary. They aren't sure what to do so they sit on the closest bench. After a minute Father O'Brian stands and turns. He looks at Bob, Crab and Christopher and says, "Hey guys, what can I do for you today?" Bob says, "We need to talk to you about something. You'll probably think that we're having DT'S or something, but I promise it's real." Father O'Brian sits on the bench beside Bob and says, "Ok, I'm all ears and I will keep an open mind. Us priest are good about that you know." Bob tells him about the spots and about the little girl. He also tells him that he was a doctor before he became a bum. Christopher is listening with his mouth hanging open like he can't believe what he's hearing. Father O'Brian listens quietly until Bob is finished. He is thinking that he could intervene but as he looks at these three homeless children of God, wanting to do this important mission, he thinks "they need this." So he asks, "What are you going to do about it?"Bob tells him that they want to get a note into Jack Johnson's pocket and that they are going to get Christopher to put it there. Bob says, "We need paper, pen and prayer." Father O'Brian says, "Prayer first." They all bow their head and the Father leads a prayer for a successful mission. They then go into his office and he lets Bob sit behind his desk and write the note. The others stand around as he writes ----- Mr. Johnson, You probably don't remember me, but I am the bum that crashed your assembly in the park. Everyone calls me Bob. Before my life took a turn for the worst I was a successful doctor, not that it matters anymore. I have discovered that I have developed this ability to see deadly illness. I do not know how it happened but I have found my insights to be true in a couple of instances that I have followed up. I see spots and shadows on people's bodies that show where there is something wrong with them. I have seen a dark spot on your daughters head leading me to believe that there may be something seriously wrong with her brain. The spots that I see vary in shades with the darker being more imminent. Your daughter's is getting darker. You have to take your daughter to the doctor and have them do a computed tomography aka CT. Please do this because her condition is getting worst. She will most likely die if you do not do this. You need to take her as soon as possible. You do not have much time. I am informing you because even though I do not practice medicine anymore, it is still in me to help people. Sincerely, Bob. He picks up the envelope that the Father had lain out on the desk and he put the note in it. He seals it, writes Jack Johnson on the front of it and hands it to Christopher. Christopher looks at him and says, "What do I do with this?" Bob replies, "Ok, here's the deal. We have to find out where Mr. Johnson will be speaking next, Father will you help us?" Father O'Brian shakes his head, "I'll look online and see where he will be." "Ok, the way I think it may work is, Crab, you and I will cause a distraction. Christopher you will slip in and put the note in Mr. Johnson's pocket." Christopher rolls his eyes and says, "All right, and call me Chris." And then he grins. He has gotten caught up in the excitement. Crab asks, "What kind of distraction are you talking about?" Bob grins real big and asks, "Do you know how to do the hula?" Crab shakes his head and says, "No way. You're not going to make me shake and shimmy." They can't help but laugh just thinking about Crab doing the hula. Father O'Brian says, "Hey, I have some hula skirts from a luau that you two can use. Bob says, "You're kidding." Father O'Brian says, "No, that would be distracting and I have a little CD player and a CD with hula music on it too. I think you should wear the skirts." They all laugh at this new development. Father O'Brian says, "Let me look online and see where he will be and when." As he looks at the computer screen he says, "Hum, it looks like his next stop will be at the fairgrounds day after tomorrow. Is that soon enough?" Bob replies, "It will have to be."

They all put back bus fare so that on the day that Mr. Johnson is suppose to be at the fair, Bob, Crab and Chris can all take the city bus there.

On that day they get there a little early so they can find a place to set up their distraction. They have a recorder with Hawaiian music on it and Father O'Brian even had an extra little speaker so they can make it loud. Bob and Crab both hit the wine hard on the way there to give themselves some extra courage. They are both pretty drunk already. People start gathering and Chris finds an inconspicuous place to blend in. Bob and Crab sneak off into the bushes to take another swig a couple of times before it starts. When Mr. Johnson is walking toward the soap box stage Bob and Crab yank the grass skirts up and turn the tape player on, they already have it up full blast and him and Crab start swiveling their hips around doing the hula. Mr. Johnson stops where he is at and stares surprised. Everyone starts laughing and pointing. Chris moves swiftly and unnoticed by Mr. Johnson slipping the note into his pocket. Mr. Johnson's body guards start moving toward Bob and Crab while they start gathering their stuff and running off. They are laughing and yelling, "Aloha" as they go.

Jack Johnson arrives home that evening and finds his wife Barbara in the parlor. "Hi, Honey. How was your day?" "Oh, fine. My sister came over and we had a nice visit. How about you?" Jack answered, "There was a big crowd. That's always a good sign." He walks over to a little bar in the corner to make a drink. "Do you want one?" She says, "I'll have the usual." He pours her a glass of white wine and makes himself a bourbon and coke. He takes the glasses over to the sofa where she is sitting at one end and hands her the glass of wine and sits at the other end. He leans back on the sofa and sighs loudly. "I'm worn out." He takes a big drink and then raises up long enough to put it on the coffee table in front of the sofa. "Funny thing happened though. You know that bum that caught me coming off of the platform in the park. He was at the fair today doing the hula to Hawaiian music. Craziest thing I have ever seen. Him and this other bum. They had skirts on and everything. I guess they were trying to steal the show. Jeff and Paul were on it though, they ran them off." Jack reaches into his pocket for a cigarette and feels the envelope. He pulls it out along with his cigarettes. "What's this?" he says as he puts the pack of cigarettes on the sofa beside him. He turns the envelope in his hand and sees that his name is written on it and then he opens it and pulls the piece of paper out and reads it. "What in the world?" Barbara asks, "What is it?" Jack says, "Somehow this was put in my pocket. It says that something is wrong with Jenny." He hands it over to Barbara and she reads it. She looks at Jack and says, "Do you think that bum may have put it into your pocket? You know he was yelling something about Jenny before." Jack says, "I don't know how. He didn't get close enough." They sit quietly for a minute and Barbara says, "I guess it wouldn't hurt to take Jenny and have them check her out. I know it doesn't make any sense but what would it hurt." Jack says, "Yeah, it wouldn't hurt. I'm going to give this to my guys and have them track down that bum so I can talk to him.

Bob, Crab and Chris went back to the church to take the hula skirt, CD player and CD back to Father O'Brian. They told him about everything laughing the whole time. When they left they were still laughing and told Father O'Brian aloha too. They had to work extra hard to get their cans for wine, but Bob had a little extra change left from the day he found the aluminum wheel. That evening Bob, Crab and Chris all met at the mission for supper. Chris kept asking him questions about the spots, even asking if they had any. Bob told Chris that he doesn't have any and Crab didn't ask. He seemed quiet, like he was thinking. That evening when they get back to their alley, there is an extra box. As they walk up Chris sticks his head out and says, "Hey guys, hope you don't mind me moving into the neighborhood. Us being such a good team and all." Bob and Crab both laugh and say, "Sure, Sure. Nice to have ya." That evening Chris joins them as they have their evening drink and conversation. The next morning they all go to the mission for breakfast and then split up to make their rounds. Bob and Crab to their can hunt and Chris to his panhandling and pocket picking. That evening they all meet at the bridge.

All of them are standing around the barrel. Crab and Chris are already there as well as Maggie, Tom, and J.J. Bob says as he walks up, "Hey you screwballs how's everybody tonight." He notices then that some of them look like they have been crying. Crab says, "Rowdy died." Bob felt like he wanted to cry too. They stand around a little while, everyone somber. Maggie is sniffling now and then. Bob says, "I'm going home." As he turns to go Crab and Chris both say that they'll walk with him. They don't say much on the way. When they get back to their alley they all sit by the wall and drink their wine and talk. Crab asks, "Did you know that Rowdy was going to die?" Bob tells him, "No, I just knew that he was really sick because his spot was dark. He just gets quiet again. Bob looks closely at Chris and asks, "How did you end up out here anyway? What are you twelve?" Chris looks offended. "I'm fourteen and I can take care of myself." Bob says," I didn't mean anything by it, but where are your parents?" You have to admit you are sort of young to be out here. Everybody gotta be a kid sometime." "I was a kid when I was nine. After that I grew up." They sat quietly for a few minutes and Chris started talking. "My father left when I was a baby and my Mama stayed until I was nine. I woke up one morning and she hadn't come home. I waited for her to come back. The landlord started knocking on the door wanting the rent and I didn't answer. He finally used his key. The first time he came I hid, but the next time I didn't. I was hungry. He called the police and next thing I know I'm in foster care. I went to three in three years. I ran away from the third one. The man there liked kids in the wrong way." They sat quietly for a couple more minutes and he said, "I miss having a home sometimes, but I don't want to go back into foster care." After sitting a couple of more minutes, Crab snores real loud and Bob and Chris look at each other and laugh. Bob reaches over and shakes Crab and tells him, "Time to go in Crab." He growls and says, "Ok, Ok, I'm going." They all go to their boxes and call it a night

The next morning they wake up with Jeff and Paul waiting for them. After describing them to Father O'Brian he had told them where to find Bob and Crab. They told Father O'Brian that they weren't going to hurt them and showed him their

Identification. They told him that Mr. Jack Johnson just wanted to talk to them. Bob and Crab started crawling out of their boxes at the same time on this morning and when they saw Jeff and Paul they start going back in. Paul said, "Whoa there, we just need to talk." Bob and Crab ease back out looking suspiciously at the two huge guys standing over them looking down. Bob stands up and Crab inches over to the wall and pulls himself up too and limps over to where Bob is. Bob and Crab both have the shakes. They reach inside their boxes and pull out their bottles and each take a big drink. That calms them some. They look at the men and Bob asks, "So, what's the deal?" The smaller of the two 'that isn't really small' says, "Mr. Johnson wants to talk to you about what happened at the fair day before yesterday. He sent us to get you. We need you to come with us." Bob looked at Crab and ask, "So, what do ya think ole pal? Should we go with these goons? No offense intended. We don't know your name so I decided to name you Big Goons." Crab snorts and slugs Bob in the arm and says, "You gonna get us killed." Bob says, "I guess we can spare an hour or two." They turn around and wave their hands indicating that they should follow. Bob looks at Chris's box and sees him peek out and then he crawls out and follows them. Parked in front of the alley is a big black limousine and the goons open the door for them to get in. Bob, Crab and Chris all climb in and are looking around in awe. The goons sit on the opposite side from them. When the limo starts moving the larger of the two says, "So you will stop calling us goons, I'm Paul and this is Jeff." They just nod their heads.

After a while the limo pulls up to a big iron gate with pillars on each side. The gate opens and they drive down a long tree lined driveway to a beautiful colonial mansion. There are steps in front and huge pillars. When they stop the chauffer gets out and opens their doors for them. All five of them walk up to the front door. Bob and Crab with Chris in the middle in front. When they reach the door Jeff rings the bell. After just seconds the door is opened by a housekeeper. Jeff tells her Mr. Johnson requested a meeting with these three guys. She looks at Bob, Chris, and Crab and says, "Come on in. I'll tell Mr. Johnson that you are here." They look around in wonder.

Everything is beautiful and expensive. There are chandeliers and a spiral staircase. The housekeeper comes back and says, "He'll see you in the parlor." They follow the housekeeper to the parlor. Mr. Johnson stands when they enter and says, "Good evening fellows. How are you this morning?" Bob and Crab both mumble that they are fine and Chris just looks at him suspiciously and says nothing. He asks, "Would you like coffee or something to drink?" Bob says, "We brought our own" and raises up his paper bag wrapped wine bottle. Crab pulls his out too. He looks at Chris and he just shakes his head no. "Alright then have a seat and let's talk." Bob and Crab look at the nice furniture and they both say, "That's alright. We'll stand." Mr. Johnson notices then how dirty their clothes are. Paul and Jeff appear out of nowhere with wood chairs. Bob and Crab sigh in relief and Chris just looks on angrily. Mr. Johnson doesn't look fazed at all. They all sit down and Bob says, "Mr. Johnson, I know why you wanted to see us. You want to decide if I'm crazy or not. I assure you that I am not. My life just turned on me." Mr. Johnson just says, "Would you tell me your story? My wife took our daughter to the doctor and they discovered a blood vessel that was getting ready to bust. She would have died if we hadn't taken her when we did. She is in the hospital now. They went in and stopped that from happening and they expect her to make a complete recovery. I don't know how you knew."

Bob looked at Mr. Johnson and saw a kindness in his eyes and he didn't know why he was doing it but he started talking and didn't stop until he had told this man his whole story. He told him about his child that he had lost, about his wife, about his successful career as a doctor and he told him about the spots. Mr. Johnson just listened quietly. He didn't look like he thought Bob was crazy or lying. He looked like he believed him. After a few minutes he said, "I want to do something for you. I don't think anybody has done anything good for you in a while. If you could have anything, what would it be?" It didn't take any time for Bob to come up with an answer. I want him to have a home he said pointing to Chris. Not a foster home, but a real home where he'll know that he is safe. His name is Chris." Mr. Johnson says, "Nice to meet you young man."

Chris says angrily, "Don't I have anything to say about this? I can take care of myself." Then he just got quiet. Jack was thinking, 'He looks like a scared kid. It broke his heart. He looked at Crab and asks him what he would want and he told him he would want the same thing. Mr. Johnson couldn't believe the generosity of these two homeless guys. "Ok then, I got this." Mr. Johnson reached into his pocket and pulled out some bills. He gave each of them a hundred and stuck the rest back into his pocket. Chris still hadn't said anything, but he took the money and Bob and Crab took it without even thinking. Even after taking the money Bob still says, "You don't have to give us this money Mr. Johnson." He replied, "Yes I do. I really want to. So you have to take it and call me Jack." he looks at his watch and says, "I have to go to a meeting at ten and then I'm going to do some checking around and I will meet you guys at evening meal at the mission. Is that alright?" Bob says, "That will work. We'll watch for you." He takes them back out to the limo and he tells the driver to take them anywhere they need to go and that he'll drive himself to the meeting.

Bob and Crab asks the limo driver to drive them through their usual neighborhood and they roll down the windows and wave at everybody that they know and then they get him to drop them at the store near the mission. Chris is quiet, like he is thinking during all of this. They go in and get themselves three bottles each. Chris buys himself a coke and some candy. This just reminds Bob and Crab that he is just a kid. When they go to pay for it with their hundred dollar bills the clerk looks surprised and says, "Looks like you boys came into some money. And you, I went to the doctor and he informed me that I am diabetic. I don't know how you knew it, but thanks. He said that you may have saved my life." Bob just smiled and looked at Crab and Chris and winked. They left the store and went around the corner to put their bottles up and to take a swig. Chris mumbled that he had to run and left. Bob and Crab look at each other and shrug their shoulders. They are enjoying not having to scavenge for their wine for a change. They go on to the mission to talk to Father O'Brian. They find him as usual praying and sit on the front bench again. After a minute or two he stands and turns around and says, "Hey, guys." Bob asks, "Talk to any really big guys lately?" Father O'Brian looks embarrassed and says, "Well, you see, it's like this, they said they weren't going to hurt you and I was thinking that it wouldn't hurt for you to talk to Mr. Johnson." He chuckled nervously. "I take it that they found you. How did it go?" Bob says, "They found us alright." Crab shakes his head and says, "Yeah, they did." Bob says, "He's going to help us find Chris a home." Father O'Brian looks up with his hands together in prayer and says, "Thank you, Lord all mighty. Thank you." And he looks at Bob and says, "My heart has been hurting for Chris for a long time and God has answered my prayers." Bob says, "He is coming to the evening meal to talk to us. I just hope that Chris will go for it. There is still time for him." Father O'Brian says, "Amen." By this time it is already close to time to start lining up for lunch sandwiches. Bob and Crab go back out of the Church side and go over to the mission side and get in line for a sandwich. They get a sandwich and go about their usual routine. That evening they get in the supper line. They keep looking for Chris. About then Jack's limousine pulls up to the curb, the driver gets out and comes around and opens the back door and Jack Johnson steps out. He thanks his driver and gives him instructions and turns and looks at the line. He spots Bob and Crab and walks over to where they are in line. "Hey guys, how's it going?" Everyone is looking on in wonder. "Would you mind if I had dinner with you this evening?" Bob and Crab both shake their heads and say, "Sure", and "Yeah" and get in line behind Crab. Nobody complains even though everyone knows that there is no skipping allowed. He whispers to them, "Have you seen him" and Bob whispers back, "Not yet." They all look around then. They see him coming around the corner headed toward the line. Bob yells, "Hey, Chris come over here a minute." Chris looks confused, but comes over to where they are. Jack tells him, "Here you can get in line in front of me." Chris looks younger than his fourteen years. He looks Jack in the face for the first time and tells him, "I'm going to trust you, I don't know why, but I am." Jack looks at Chris and his heart breaks. He is small for his size and his clothes are all dirty and torn.

His hair is shoulder length and looks dirty. He has a skinned place on his cheek and a scar on his forehead. He could tell that he's living a hard life. They go through the line and get their food and they see a table that's empty, that must have been Father O'Brian's doing. There is a sign on it that reads "Reserved for Jack Johnson." Bob and Crab look at each other and shrug their shoulders and sit on one side. Jack says, "Come on Chris. He sits on the same side as Jack. They start eating. Bob hadn't realized how hungry he was and by the way that Crab was putting it down he was hungry too. They hadn't eaten anything since their sandwich at lunch. While they are eating, Jack starts talking to Chris. It starts out pretty formal, but before long they seem to be getting along like old pals. He tells Chris that he wants to help him. He says he wants to find him a home 'not a foster home' a real home with a good family. Chris acts tough, but he has a yearning look on his face while Jack is talking about him having a home. He tells him that he is going to find him a home if it kills him. Jack asks Bob and Crab, "What would you two want more than anything? There is no real way that I can repay you for saving my daughter's life. That is priceless." They are both thinking. Bob says, "My life is not my on anymore. I would like to climb out of this bottle." They all knew what he meant. Crab says, "I wouldn't mind sleeping in a bed again, but I gotta have my wine for the pain." They all sit quietly for a moment and then Jack says, "I would like all three of you to meet me here tomorrow. That is if you don't mind. I want to help you." They all three shake their heads yes. Jack stands up and says, "I'll see you tomorrow" and leaves.

They all left dazed. They walked out of the mission together. When they are outside Bob says, "What do ya think of that?" Crab is shaking his head from side to side and replies, "I just don't know." Chris is sniffling and says, "I don't think the guy knows what he's talking about. These goody two shoes think they know how to do stuff and they don't have any idea." Bob needs to think. "I'll see ya'll later." He looks around at all of the spots on people and walks off. Crab and Chris take off in different directions.

This gets Bob thinking about his past life before he started drinking. Before he married and lost his baby girl. 'I use to have a good life. A long time ago. He looks down at his hands and notices that they are shaking so he steps off into an alley and takes a couple of good swigs from his bottle. Throughout the whole day he thinks about his past. He hadn't done that in a long time. Usually the wine makes him forget. Bob, Crab and Chris don't see each other until that night when they meet in their alley and all three sit by the wall. They are quiet at first, but then they start talking about what it would be like to live in a house again. To have a life different from the one that they are living now. They start dreaming again. After awhile they all crawled into their boxes for the night.

The next morning they go to the mission and try to act normal, but they are all very distracted. They sit together at breakfast, but don't talk much. Too much has happened in their lives for them to believe good things could happen for them again. When they go their separate ways they don't say anything about the evening meal.

Jack Johnson goes home after talking to Bob, Crab and Chris and talks to his wife. He describes Chris and tells her how it hurts his heart to see the child homeless. He tells her that this child needs a family. One that would be patient and not let him down. She gives him that look that says she's on board. First he says that he wants her to meet him. He tells her that she can come to the mission with him. Their little girl was a miracle and they had not been able to have any more children. They had been talking for years about adopting another child 'one that needed them.'

That evening when they all met at the mission everybody had a good time. Barbara fell in love with Chris and he seemed to like her too. She enjoyed meeting Bob and Crab too. When they left Jack told Bob that he would catch him in a couple of days. He didn't tell him that he needed the time to do research on everything. Bob was disappointed because he thought he was going to find a home for Chris. Bob, Crab and Chris were sort of melancholy as they made their way to the bridge. The usual group was there. When they saw them coming they started picking on them saying things like, "Oh, so now you're going to hang with us lower class people." "I hope we don't mess up your reputation" laughing good naturedly. They didn't tell them anything about what was really going on. Bob tells them that the guy is running for senate so he is just trying to get votes by hanging out with homeless people. Crab and Chris just shake their heads in agreement. The subject changes after that and after awhile they go back to their alley.

The next morning they get up as usual and go to eat breakfast. They don't talk about Jack Johnson. Bob goes about his day. He is still seeing spots on everybody, mostly shadows. He does see a darker spot on people sometimes but, he doesn't say anything. It makes him feel guilty to not help but he knows that they won't believe him. He day dreams about being a doctor again and being able to help people with the spots. He collects his cans and cashes them in for wine. He wants to hold on to the money that Jack gave him for emergency money.

On the third day after they had talked to Jack, they woke up with Jeff and Paul standing outside their boxes. Bob sticks his head out and says, "Well, lookie here. It's the goons, I mean Jeff and Paul. Sorry guys old habits ya know." About then Crab sticks his head out, his hair is sticking out all over his head and with his wondering eye, he looks pretty funny. Jeff and Paul can't help but laugh. Crab says, "Not you two again." Jeff says, "Good morning guys, Mr. Johnson sent us to get you. That is if you don't mind. He wants to talk to you about something." They look at each other and Bob says, "Chris, wake up." After a couple of seconds Chris sticks his head out of his box and looks suspiciously around. Bob tells him, "You need to come with us." Chris looks like he is going to refuse, but then he slowly shakes his head and crawls out and stands up. Bob says, "You won't get hurt. I promise." He doesn't understand himself why he is trusting Jack, just a feeling. He crawls out of his own box and stands. Chris looks so raggedy. He pulls his baggy pants up and combs his hair with his fingers and says, "Ok, I'm ready." They all follow Jeff and Paul out of the alley and they climb into the limousine.

They arrive at the mansion and the housekeeper lets them in and tells them that Mr. and Mrs. Johnson are in the parlor waiting for them. The housekeeper announces them and they enter the parlor. Jack and Barbara both stand as they enter. They are both smiling and start walking over to them with their hands outstretched, Jack says, "Hi guys, it's so nice of you to come. We are so excited to talk to you about something." Let's go to the dining room. The cook has made us some breakfast and we can eat while we talk." Their eyes light up because they are hungry, last time they had missed breakfast. They all go into the dining room. There is a large table with a beautiful chandelier over it. Jack waves them to one end and they all sit down. He starts out telling them that him and Barbara had thought long and hard about their situation and had come up with an idea. It would all depend on what they wanted to do with their lives. Jack and Barbara both looked at Chris and Jack says, "We have talked about it and we would love for you to come live with us. We have wanted a son for a long time. Barbara can't have any more children and as we see it, we need you and we figured you maybe wouldn't mind living in a house with a family. We want you to be part of our family." Barbara says, "I would love for you to live here. We talked to Jenny and she says she wouldn't' mind having a brother." She wanted to meet you but she's still in the hospital." Chris looked stunned. After a few seconds Jack says, "We don't have to have an answer right away. I promise that we will be good to you and that we will provide everything that you need to accomplish your every dream. Just think about it."

They turned then and ask, Bob and Crab, "Have you two ever thought about sobering up?" They both looked panicked, like they might run out of the house. Then they seem to calm down. Bob speaks first, "I've found that since I have been seeing these spots I want to help people again. I don't think that I'm too far gone. I wonder how hard it would be to reinstate my license to practice." Jack says, "I guess you know that first you'll have to clean up your act. That means a rehab program. I will pay for your program and do everything that I can to help you start working again." At this point Bob has tears running down his face and he is shaking his head "Yes." He then looks at Crab and says, "Well?" Crab says, "I have so much pain in my leg that I can't stop drinking." Jack says,

"We'll work on that too. I'll find the best doctor there is to see if we can't do something to make it tolerable. They can't work on you if you're drunk. Same deal as Bob." He looks scared but he reaches his hand out and says, "I would like to introduce myself. My name is Michael Lake." They all looked surprised. Bob didn't even know his real name. Jack says, "Nice to meet you Michael Lake. I don't know what kind of work you would like to do. I think you would probably be eligible for disability. Barbara can help you apply. I will let you three think about these options and let me know what you think. Take as long as you need." They finish eating talking all the while about what they might expect from rehab and about Chris going to school. They tell him that they could get him a tutor to catch him up or he could be home schooled. It would be up to him. After awhile Jack has his limo driver take them back. When they get back to their alley they sit lined up against the wall. Chris says, "I'm going to do it." Bob says, "Me too." Crab says, "What the hell, me too" They all laugh. They spend the day goofing off. They hang out at the river talking and Bob and Crab drinking their wine. They know it will be their last.

The next morning they get up early and go to Jack's. They stand nervously at the gate and push the buzzer. The housekeeper opens the gate from inside the house. As they are walking up the driveway to the mansion Bob says, "Well, we're climbing out of the bottles. Crab asks, "Do I have any spots?" Bob replies "Not a one." Crab grins and keeps walking. When Bob woke up that morning there were no more spots. Whatever it was had passed.

THE END

26

Get Out of my Head!

"I control everything and they don't even realize it."

Dr. Frond had been researching this idea for ten years and he finally figured out how to make it work. They needed to get into people's heads. This device would send continuous subliminal messages to the brain telling the person that they are very hungry and need to eat or they will die. It's brilliant. He had developed the devices to be installed into people's homes and they would install cameras that would monitor their every move and they would watch and take notes.

Becky Peterson enters her home after a long day at her job as a vet at the animal shelter. Her house is in a nice neighborhood. It is brick with a manicured lawn and flower beds. Critter and Spike meet her at the door. Critter's a huge tom cat that roars a meow at her as he wraps around her legs demanding food. She brought him home from the shelter when he was a kitten. Behind him is a little terrier with three legs named Spike. He was found in an alley and brought in with a severely damaged leg. That's the problem with being a veterinarian; you end up bringing your work home. She also has a snake named Oscar and a bird named Joey. She goes about feeding all of her fury and feathered family. Then she puts frozen vegetarian lasagna in the oven and jumps in the shower. When she gets out of the shower she can smell her dinner. Her food has ten more minutes. She picks up her mail and flips through it as Spike comes in through the doggy door. She sees a letter from a home security company. It isn't addressed to resident so she opens it. Inside is an advertisement for a free installation of home security if you called and gave them the code on the letter. She put it down with the other mail, just bills and such. The oven dinged signaling that her food is done. She eats her dinner in front of the TV watching the news where there is a report of burglaries in her neighborhood. She thinks about the ad and decides to give them a call the next day.

Dr. Frond met with the federal agents. He is so excited about his invention that he can hardly contain himself. He told them that the device is ready to be tested. They just need certain types of subjects. They needed very health conscious persons that exercise, eat right and basically do everything in moderation. They would have to be financially and emotionally stable. They would have to be single and independent. The plan would be to see if they could control the eating habits of the subjects. This device will send messages to the brain that tells the person that they are ravenously hungry to the point that they could eat themselves to death. They would want to use the most stable subjects that they could find. If it works on them it will be certain to work on the weaker ones. By doing this they could make their enemies overweight and unhealthy. They would eventually eat themselves to death. This could also make their enemies thin and weak. The possibilities are endless. They could use this to make Americans healthier of course too. They could eventually control other aspects of their enemy's lives and habits. They need to find people that would be hard to brainwash to experiment on. They had special investigators to find the subjects that they needed.

The next morning Becky is up early dressed in her workout suit which is a t-shirt and jogging pants. She opens up the doggy door and puts food and water down for Critter and Spike. They know which bowl belongs to which. It could be that the tom cat is very big and loud and the terrier is older and mellower that makes for such a respectful relationship between the two. She gives Oscar and Joey fresh water and food. It is sort of disturbing feeding mice to Oscar but that's what he has to have. She does her thirty minutes on the treadmill, some sit ups, and some reps with her ten pound weights. Then she jumps in the shower and puts on some jeans and a blouse. She has a bowl of oatmeal with blueberries and a glass of orange juice for breakfast. When she's ready to go she grabs her purse and briefcase and then she sees the envelope about home security and puts it in her purse. She tells all of her animal kids "Be good" and goes to work.

When she reaches the clinic she checks her appointment schedule for the morning and pulls the files. It's only 7:30. Her first appointment is at 8:00, a golden retriever needing annual shots. The receptionist arrives at a quarter till. By then Becky had already made coffee. She doesn't drink coffee but Sarah does. About the time Sarah gets her coffee and gets settled in. Mrs. Thomas and her dog Mickey arrives. The morning flies by with one pet after another. Becky had to cast a leg and remove a splinter but mostly it was checkups and shots. Around 2:00 she finally has time to take a break. She sits at her desk and has a yogurt and a pear. She always keeps a bowl of fruit on her desk for herself and Sarah. She thinks about the envelope in her purse and decides to call about the security system. With the burglaries in her neighborhood she isn't feeling secure with just her and her animals. They give her a deal that she can't refuse. Only fifty dollars a month. Usually the installation cost one hundred and fifty dollars. The equipment is usually three hundred dollars, but they are letting her have everything she needs installed for ninety nine dollars. There would be alarms on all of the doors and windows that would let her know that someone is breaking in. And they would install cameras outside her front door and in her back yard. When they installed the equipment they would show her how to set the alarm and disarm it.

One year after Dr. Frond talked to the agents about the test, they had the project organized. They had found their test subjects. Twenty persons of excellent health and status. They were selected from all over the United States. They needed a variety of subjects that are different sexes, ethnicity, cultures and personalities. They chose different ways to get into their homes, home security installations, phone, cable, internet, even bottle water delivery. Whatever the situation called for. They installed the boxes that would send messages to the brain. They put tiny cameras in the houses so that they could watch the results and turn the brain feeds on and off as needed. That way they can control the dosage of brain feed that is given and also turn it off when others are around. It is all remote and will be controlled from other locations. This new device should make the cravings so overwhelming that even the strongest person will be unable to resist.

Patti Dawson enters her luxury condominium after a long day at her studio. She is owner of five photography studios in five major cities. Her studios have a reputation for outstanding quality. She lays her briefcase on the table beside the door and yells, "Mia, I'm home." Mia is her housekeeper and friend. She has worked for Patti for twelve years and before that she had worked for her parents. Mia came through the door that leads to the kitchen and greeted Patti saying "How was your day kid?" Mia had been in Patti's life for so long that she treats her like one of her own children. "Same old thing." "My sales rep Gabby is getting married. You remember her don't you? "She's been working with us forever." Mia says, "Yeah, I do. Nice lady." "Have they set a date yet?" Patti shakes her head, "No, he just proposed last night. I'm going to work out for about an hour before supper." Mia says, "I'm making smoked salmon with cucumber salad. It will be about two hours." Patti turns to leave and says, "Ok, thanks, Mama Mia." Mia just laughs and shakes her head. This has been an ongoing joke between them. Patti works out for the hour and then she showers and changes into her lounging pajamas. She goes into her home office thinking that she might check her email before supper, but when she tries to get online, she can't. She checks all of her connections and doesn't see anything wrong. Mia always joins Patti for meals. She can't treat her like anything but family. While they are eating Patti tells her about the internet problem. Mia says that she will call the computer guy first thing in the morning. Mia only stays until six o'clock so after they eat she puts the dishes in the dishwasher and starts it. She always empties it first thing in the morning. The next morning she calls like she said she would and they immediately send a technician out.

In a meeting about the experiment Dr. Frond is questioned about the moral issues that some people would see in what they are doing. He tells them that in his opinion it is all for the greater good. He also informs them that when it is over they will help the subjects take the weight off again. That is why they need such healthy persons for the program in the beginning. They will be closely monitored and after they have their results they will reverse the message to allow them to regain their health. This is the only way to do it. The subjects knowing what is happening would affect the results of the experiment. They all agreed. Dr. Frond has a strange gleam in his eyes. He is thinking "I control everything and they don't even realize it."

The day after the home security system is installed Becky awakes feeling hungrier than she has ever felt in her life. She grabs an apple out of the bowl that she keeps on her counter before she even lets Spike out or takes care of her other pets. She finishes her apple and eats a banana as she gets on her treadmill. She keeps it in her living room. She thinks "I might need some vitamins" as she walks on her treadmill eating a banana. She does her usual thirty minutes and is starving by the time she gets off of it. She makes herself some oatmeal with blueberries, toast and a glass of milk. A large breakfast for her. When she is done she still feels like she can eat more, but thinks "I've had enough, I have to get out of here". She spent so much time eating that she didn't have time for the rest of her workout. When she arrives at work she still feels that unsatisfied hunger but it eases up the longer she is there. Eating so much earlier made her feel a little draggy but she starts taking care of her patients and soon it is out of her head. That evening after a long day she stops and picks up a vegetarian pizza on her way home. When she arrives home she goes through her usual routine of taking care of the animals all of the time thinking about the pizza. She decides to postpone her workout until after she eats. She ends up eating the whole pizza and lying on her couch with a stomach ache. Even with the stomach ache she is craving food. She thinks "What's happening to me?" She decides to call her doctor and make an appointment the next day.

The next day Becky wakes up starving again. She foregoes her usual routine, eats all morning and skips her treadmill workout. She just feels too bogged down to do any of her workout. She grabs her briefcase and makes herself go on to work. When she gets to work she's all sluggish but she checks her appointment schedule and pulls all of the files she'll need and she makes coffee. This time she decides to have a cup with sweetener and creamer. Totally against her regimen. She hopes this will perk her up. She does perk up after a little while. Around ten o'clock she takes a few minutes and calls her doctor. They tell her that they can get her in the next day. Her hunger feelings lessen throughout the day. She skips lunch since she ate so much earlier. By the end of the day she's feeling like herself again. When she gets home she starts feeling incredibly hungry again and figures it's because even though she ate a lot that morning she did skip lunch. She fights the hunger feelings and makes herself get on the treadmill to make up for not exercising that morning. After walking on the treadmill, the hunger hit her like a hammer. She had to have food. She was shaking and salivating. She goes to her kitchen and opens the cabinets and grabs a box of crackers out, tears into the box and starts stuffing them into her mouth all the time thinking "What's wrong with me". She opens her refrigerator and starts pulling everything out. She drinks milk right out of the jug. She eats everything she can find. She finally feels like she can't fit anything else into her stomach. She is miserable. She runs to her bathroom and throws up and falls asleep on her couch.

She awakens later and stumbles to the bathroom and takes a shower. When she gets out of the shower, she falls into her bed still sick with a stomach ache. The next morning she gets up early. Having digested all that she had eaten she is once again hungry. She makes herself a huge bowl of cereal with a banana in it, toast, and a big glass of juice. When she is done with that she eats a whole package of the crackers that she had opened the day before. Even Critter and Spike are looking at her funny. She doesn't feel like doing her workout and figures the best thing for her to do is to get out of the house so she won't eat any more. Her doctor's appointment isn't until one o'clock so she goes to the clinic and takes care of her morning appointments. She had gotten Sarah to reschedule the rest of the day's appointments. At twelve o'clock she leaves. When she arrives for her doctor's appointment she doesn't have to wait long before she is called back. She has been seeing Dr. Bally for a couple of years now and she really likes him. "Good evening Becky, what brings you here today?" She tells him about her feeling so hungry all of the time and that she can't seem to control her eating. He tells her that maybe some vitamins would help, but he will run some blood test just to check everything out. "I'll check your thyroid, blood glucose, and iron and such." "How can I stop my eating? I don't feel like I have any control over it." Dr. Bally asks, "Has anything happened in your life that has you stressed or depressed?" "No I feel fine except for the hunger." He looks at her for a moment and then asks her to get up on the exam table. He listens to her heart and lungs. Takes her blood pressure. And he tells her, "You are probably one of healthiest patients I have. You know though, with you being a vegetarian, sometimes people on this diet miss some of the vitamins and minerals that they need." I recommend that you start taking a multi-vitamin." She shakes her head and says, "Ok." As he helps her off of the table he tells her, "Alright, they will give you a blood work order at the reception desk." "You can just take it next door and have it done today if you like and I will call you in a couple of days with the results." "Thanks, Dr. Bally, I'll talk to you in a couple of days then." They shake hands and she leaves. She has the blood work done and on the way home she stops at the drug store and picks up multi-vitamins.

When Patti Dawson arrives home from work the day after they had talked about the internet being out, Mia meets her at the door. "Hey Kiddo, the computer guy was here. Real weirdo. You're up and running again though." "Oh, that's great." What's for supper?" "I am making lemon chicken, steamed broccoli, and salad." "That sounds great." I'm going to work out." Mia tells her "Your supper should be done at five." That gives Patti a couple of hours. She does her workout, showers and then she goes into her office until supper. They sit down to supper as usual and afterwards Mia cleans up and leaves. Patti is in her office doing some research on photography equipment when she starts feeling really hungry. She never allows herself to eat after six. She fights it off for about ten minutes and just can't take it anymore. She thinks "Maybe some little something won't hurt" She goes into the kitchen. It's all cleaned up and the dishwasher is still running. She thinks, "I don't know what's going on with me I just ate supper half an hour ago" "Maybe I need desert" She looks in the freezer and sees that there is orange sherbet. She gets herself a bowl out of the cabinet and a spoon out of a drawer and makes herself a bowl. She eats it in a couple of minutes and still wants more. She puts more in her bowl and eats it too. Then she just looses it and eats all of the rest of the sherbet right out of the container. She looks in her pantry and sees cookies. She takes them out and eats the whole package. She's feeling pretty guilty by this time and has a stomach ache. She goes back to her office and tries to work but feels horrible and ends up going up to her room and lying down. She can't believe it but she is still craving food. She falls asleep with her stomach hurting. The next morning she wakes up starving. She can't believe it with all that she had eaten the night before. She has a huge breakfast and skips her morning jog. She just can't stop eating. She forces herself to stop though and goes to work.

Dr. Frond is personally monitoring the start up of the program. He is remotely turning the brain feeds on and off as necessary. He has twenty screens set up in front of him. Each one is showing a different subjects home. He realizes that there may be a problem with one of the subjects. She has a housekeeper. That makes it hard to do the brain feeds as much as they need and she seems to be a friend and may become worried about the change. Dr. Frond decides that he will personally take care of this little glitch. This Ms. Dawson lives in Dallas. He'll take a flight out there right away and fix it. He leaves a schedule of when to turn the feeds on and off for his assistant. His assistant is a young easily influenced lab technician that he hypnotized. Dr. Frond knows that not all people see things the way that he does. They aren't as advanced in thinking as he is. He doesn't really explain what

34

he is actually doing, but the assistant is in such awe of Dr. Frond that he doesn't ask. It doesn't hurt that he is hypnotized either. He just knows that he is working with the great Dr. Frond and that the work is top secret. He calls an old associate of his in Dallas that has helped him acquire certain necessary items and arranges to get a gun equipped with a silencer. He then makes reservations for the first flight to Dallas, Texas. Once he lands he rents a car and drives to the associate's home and picks up the gun. Then he goes directly to Patti Dawson's condominium. The housekeeper most likely parked in the parking garage so he parks across the street from the exit and tries to be as inconspicuous as possible. The timing works out perfectly, he can do what he has to and fly back as quickly as possible. It is five thirty eight. The housekeeper will be coming out soon. He sits and watches. She pulls out in her little blue car. The installer had informed him about the housekeeper and told him what she drove. He didn't know then that she spent so much time with the subject or that she was actually an old friend. He pulls out and follows her. He tries not to get too close. She doesn't live far from Ms. Dawson. Her neighborhood is more middle class than her employers. She pulls into the driveway of a nice wood frame house with a screened in front porch. Dr. Frond drives by and goes around the block. Before he passes by again he stops a couple of houses up and takes a priest collar out of his pocket and puts it on. He sees that she has gone inside. All of her neighbors are inside too. He pulls in front of her house and parks. He picks up the bible that he has on the passenger seat and pats his pocket where he has his pistol with the silencer. He walks up to the screen porch and opens the door. It's unlocked. He's thinking "Some people are so trusting" He knocks on the door and after a minute she peeks out of the window. He yells through the window, "I'm Father Joseph Carson, I'm collecting money for the mission." And he smiles his brightest smile. He looks so friendly and harmless that she opens the door. He is still smiling when he raises the gun and shoots her. He then drives back toward the airport, on the way he drops the gun into a dumpster. He only has to wait one hour before he can catch a flight back. On his way to the bar he drops the bible and collar in a trash can. He is back home by the next morning.

The doctor calls Becky a couple of days after she went in and tells her that her test all came back normal. She is still eating constantly while she is at home. The only time she can relax and not eat is when she is at work. This morning she is in her bathroom after showering and steps on her scale. She has gained eleven pounds in one week. She raises her shirt up and looks at her stomach and sees that she is definitely getting a pooch. She feels like crying but she is also so hungry that she can't stand it. She dresses quickly and goes into her kitchen to see what she has. Her cupboard is almost empty. She must have eaten everything last night. She has gotten where she loses track of what all she eats. She finds some instant grits and milk. She makes the half full box of grits and finishes up the milk. She is feeling panicky and decides to stop at the store and pick up some food on her way home. She doesn't have time to work out so she goes on to the clinic.

Patti is just sick over Mia. Who would want to kill Mia? The police asked her the same thing. She decides to take a few days off from work. She stays around her house and cries a lot. She also eats a lot, nonstop actually. She just figures that this is how she is handling losing Mia. She eats until she's miserable and then cries herself to sleep. She keeps thinking "What's happening to me?" "I'm falling to pieces." She ends up taking even more time off. She stops exercising completely. After a couple of weeks of this she looks at herself in the mirror and is surprised at how much weight she has put on. She has always been in great shape. Looking in the mirror she sees that her waist is looking thick. She can pinch almost two inches. That just makes her cry again and she eats a whole half gallon of ice cream.

Dr. Frond is very pleased at how well the experiment is going. Two weeks in and they are all gaining weight. They have five subjects in Dallas, five in Los Angeles, five in New York, and five in Miami. Ten women, ten men. Four Caucasian, four

African American, four Hispanic, four Chinese, and four French. So far everyone has gained at least fifteen pounds. It's time to pick it up.

Becky goes to the grocery store and buys three hundred and fifty dollars worth in groceries. When she gets home she doesn't even get all of the groceries put up before she starts eating. She stuffs food into her mouth like a starving person. She eats like this until she can't hold anymore and then lies down in a sort of stupor. The next morning she awakens feeling just as hungry. She eats up until she has to leave. When she arrives at work she is still craving food. Usually it lightens up when she is at work but it isn't this day. She eats all of the fruit in her bowl, checks her schedule, pulls files and makes coffee at the same time. When Sarah arrives she looks at her like she hadn't ever seen her before. She notices that Dr. Peterson looks awful. She doesn't have her hair fixed and her clothes are wrinkled. She looks puffy and her complexion doesn't look good. She has also gained a lot of weight. Becky is a very attractive woman with her strawberry blond hair and blue eyes. When she tries to talk to her to find out if she is okay, she snaps at her angrily. She decides to just leave her alone for now, maybe it will pass. Becky just keeps thinking about food. She has to leave she's so hungry. She tells Sarah that she is sick and asks her to reschedule her appointments. The next day goes almost the same way except she takes food with her. She can't concentrate on anything. She ends up calling another veterinarian to cover for her while she takes some personal time off. She then closes herself up in her house and has groceries delivered. After a couple of months like this, she looks at herself in the mirror in her bathroom and sees a severely obese woman. And she cries.

Meanwhile Patti is eating constantly and picking up speed. She still hasn't returned to work. She just let her managers handle things while she takes some time off. She shuts herself in and eats. After about three months like this she had gained a hundred pounds. She looks at herself in the mirror and sees that the usual slim attractive brunette has been replaced by a seriously overweight unhealthy woman. She decides it's time to see her doctor. When she goes into her doctor's office she runs test looking for a physical cause. All of the test results come back normal. She decides that she is going to have to use self control. She doesn't believe in taking drugs because none of them are completely harmless. She goes back to her house and starts eating.

Sarah starts to really get worried about Becky. She hasn't come into the clinic for a month so she decides to go by her house and check on her. When she gets there she knocks on the door and waits. She can hear Spike barking but Becky doesn't come to the door. Her garage door is closed so she can't tell if she is there or not. She knocks again and still nothing. She is about to leave when she notices the curtain moving. She had talked to her on the phone and she had seemed ok. She decides to take a chance. She yells, "I know you're home, come on please, I need to talk to you." It works, she opens the door. Sarah can't believe how bad she looks. She has gained so much weight that she must be over three hundred pounds. She is standing there in sweat pants that look like they are stretched to full capacity and a night shirt almost as tight. There are food stains all over the front of her shirt and she is holding a sandwich in one hand. Sarah just stands there and stares. Not one to beat around the bush she says "What's going on with you?" Becky just starts crying and Sarah puts her arms around her. Becky starts blubbering "I don't know what's wrong." "I can't stop eating." "I feel horrible." Sarah leads her to the couch and they sit down. Becky tells her everything that's going on. She tells her that she has blackouts and can't remember eating or even going to the store for that matter. Spike has come up and laid his head on Becky's lap. Sarah notices unopened mail stacked on her coffee table. Most have Urgent stamped on them. Becky notices her looking and says, "I can't even concentrate enough to pay bills" Sarah asks "Have you gone to the doctor?" Becky tells her "Yes, all of my test results are normal, it's not physiological." Sarah says quietly "I hate to ask but what about psychological?" "You know me Sarah, I'm not crazy."

Dr. Frond is watching this on his monitor. Another problem to take care of. So far the program has been doing excellent. One of the subjects in Dallas has committed suicide. Zack James, he was a fitness trainer and volunteer fire fighter. Dr. Frond was able to get his total savings before he departed. At zero savings and three hundred and fifty pounds he shut himself in his garage in his running truck and died of carbon monoxide poisoning. That was the ending he needed, self destruction. Now though, he has to do something about Sarah Jones. He decided to let one of his associates take care of this one.

Sarah left with a heavy heart, telling Becky to call her if she needs anything. Her mind is racing. After Sarah leaves Becky sits on her couch looking at the stack of mail, eating her sandwich. She picks up the mail and looks through it. She notices a letter from her bank. It is also stamped urgent. She opens it without really thinking and reads ---*Ms. Peterson, We are writing this letter to inform you that there has been some unusual activity with your account. Whenever large amounts of funds are withdrawn it is our policy to send out a letter to the client to confirm their knowledge of such activity.* She looks at the second page where the statement information is and is stunned. According to this statement she has withdrawn fifty thousand dollars from her savings. She thinks, "This has got to be a mistake." She rolls off of the couch and pulls herself up. She has gotten so big. She walks over to the phone; it is a cordless, picks it up and makes her way back over to the couch. She plops down, the couch creaks and makes a cracking sound, but doesn't break. She picks up the letter and calls the bank. She talks to a clerk and tells her that she didn't withdraw this money. The clerk says that she remembers seeing her in the bank and would transfer her to the banker that she talked to while she was there. When the banker answers the phone, she introduces herself as Mary Hall and she confirms that she did help her with a large transaction. She says that Becky had told her that she was donating money to a research project and needed a cashier's check for fifty thousand dollars. She said that she showed identification, and knew all of the information concerning her account. Becky argued that it couldn't be her and the agent recommends that she come in and they could discuss it. By the time she had made it off of the couch she had forgotten about the call and the letter. She goes into the kitchen to find something to eat.

Patti stays in her house all of the time now. She has her groceries delivered and eats constantly. She also stopped taking care of herself. She stopped weighing and she stopped looking in the mirror too. Everyone assumes that she is still mourning Mia. Her friend Gabby had gotten married and gone on a long honeymoon. Patti told her that she couldn't go to the wedding because she had thrown her back out. She was really embarrassed over all of the weight that she had gained. It has been over four months since the project had started and she is at three hundred pounds. She doesn't realize it but her savings are down by one hundred thousand dollars. The brain feeds are erasing the withdrawals from her memory. She did order clothes to fit her off of the internet, usually sweats and t-shirts. She can't concentrate on anything but eating. She doesn't bathe, brush her hair or change clothes. She is losing track of time constantly. Every once in a while she thinks "What's happening to me?" She feels really depressed. She's lost control of everything.

Sarah decides to go by and check on Becky before she goes home. It's been a couple of days since she was over there. When she is leaving the clinic she has to cross the street to her car. Before she crosses she looks both ways, but when she had made it about half way a car comes out of nowhere and is heading straight at her. The car isn't even trying to stop. Right before the car hits her she dives out of the way. She lands and rolls to the curb between two parked cars. Her heart is hammering in her chest and she is breathing hard. She thinks, "Someone tried to kill me." "What the hell." She sits up and checks herself for injuries. She has a skinned knee and elbow. Her cheek hurts and she put her hand up to it and when she brings it back down and looks at it she sees blood. Not a lot though. She stands up slowly and looks around. She doesn't see any more cars coming after her so she gets her key out of her purse and has it ready. She runs around the car and gets inside as quickly as she can. She has a feeling that this has something to do with what is going on with Becky, just intuition, so she drives over to her house.

She calls on the way and tells Becky that she's coming over so when she knocks on the door she hears Spike barking and then she hears Becky walking to the door. When she opens the door it looks like she had at least changed clothes. Her hair is still unbrushed and there are stains all over her t-shirt but it is a different one. When Becky sees her, her eyes widen and she asks "What happened to you? I have first aid in the bathroom. I'll be right back." She labors out of the room and returns a minute later. She is out of breath and she plops back down onto the couch. It makes the popping and cracking sound again and Sarah thinks "it's going to break". There is food and food wrappers all around. They talk while Becky puts medicine and a bandage on Sarah's cheek where there is a small cut. They also doctor her knee and elbow. When they are done they both lean back on the couch and just lay there. Becky starts eating crackers that somehow appeared in her hands. Sarah says, "Why would someone want to kill me? I know it wasn't an accident. He didn't even try to stop. She sits up and Becky struggles up with help from Sarah. Then Sarah says, "It was a man, I saw that in the second before I got out of the way." Becky looks down at the coffee table in front of them and sees the open letter. Just from a glance she sees that it concerns money and she says "What's this?" Becky picks it up, and says "Oh yeah, I was going to check into that but for some reason it slipped my mind." Then Becky remembers, "Somehow they messed up and I ended up with fifty thousand dollars missing out of my savings account." Sarah startled said, "Becky, people don't just forget about fifty thousand dollars." "I know that you aren't struggling, but fifty thousand dollars?" "Something is going on here. I don't know what, but we need to find out." "Maybe someone has broken in here and found personal information." "Would you mind if I looked around?" Becky replies, "Sure, I don't know what good it will do, but go ahead."

First she looks at the mail on the coffee table. "Becky, do you realize that you haven't paid any of your bills?" Sarah doesn't really know what she is looking for but she goes through the apartment looking everywhere. She starts noticing wires running to cameras and boxes. "Becky, what is all of this stuff?" "I had home security installed about six or seven months ago. I really hadn't needed it much because I'm always here now." Sarah asked, "When did you start eating uncontrollably?" Becky answered distractedly, "It was about that time." Sarah says, "Humph, that's interesting." Becky asked, "Do you think that has anything to do with it?" "I don't know." And then she asked, "What would you think if I unhooked all of this and we'll see what happens?" Becky says, "Ok, I mean, I'm here all of the time now anyway." Sarah follows all of the wires and disconnects everything that she can find. She checks for batteries to make sure all power is gone and puts everything in a box she found in the garage. When she's done she says, "We need to find out about your money."

Dr. Frond is throwing a major fit. "What happened?" One of his monitors is blank. Before it went blank he saw a battered Sarah Jones having an interesting conversation with Ms. Peterson. Next thing he knows she is pulling all of the wires loose. While this is going on he is watching and saying over and over "No, No, No, this can't be happening." His mind is racing. "He doesn't know how to fix this. This isn't supposed to happen. The federal defense department doesn't know about the money he's taking. He has already acquired over a million dollars. Oh no, I've got to do damage control." He is so stunned he doesn't know where to start.

She asks Becky as respectfully as possible if she could clean up and brush her hair and then she ran out and bought her some larger size clothes. She needs something to wear to the bank so they will take her seriously. When she gets back, first thing she notices is that Becky isn't eating. She looks nice and clean and is even wearing makeup. She had gone to a specialty store that served larger size customers and found her a nice dress and matching shoes that are more like slippers. Even her feet had gotten bigger, wider anyway. Sarah waited in the living room while Becky dressed.

When they arrive at the bank Becky tells them who she is and they let her talk to the banker that they had said helped her before. Mary Hall introduces herself again and tells her that when she came in a week and a half before she had requested a cashier's check for fifty thousand dollars because she had decided to donate some money. They were surprised that she would make such a large donation, but it is her money. Becky tells her that it couldn't have been her. She wouldn't donate almost all of her savings to anybody. Mary Hall tells her that it was her, she recognizes her from when she came in before. She doesn't handle such large withdrawals often and they have to go through the safety questions and they even scan prints. She told her, "It was you." "Look I believe we still have the video from that day." "Come with me." They went to the security office in the bank. They knock on the door and a guard lets them in. The one guard sits back down in front a bank of monitors. There is another guard sitting there too. Mary Hall asked them about the video from the date they needed and one of the guards finds it and puts it in the player for them. The video is actually pretty clear and there she was. She looked horrible. She was dressed like she was in her apartment before Sarah went and bought her some more clothes. They saw her talk to a clerk and then the clerk took her to talk to the banker. She couldn't deny it. This person in the video looks exactly like her and even moves like her. Becky says, "You say you scanned my prints?" Mary hall replies, "Yes, you do remember how we put your prints into the computer when we first added this procedure to our security plan, don't you?" "We felt that it would help keep the customer's accounts safe." Sarah whispered to Becky, "Find out if the check was cashed and who it was made out to." Becky says, "So, has the check been cashed?" Mary Hall tells her that she can show her a copy of the cashed check. Becky is stunned with everything that has happened and nods and says, "Yes, please."

They go back to Mary Hall's office and she gets on her computer. She tells Becky that if she does online banking, she can look at it in there. She stands up and lets Becky sit at her computer and she logs in. She pulls up the cashier's check and sees that it is made out to Jacob Frond. Becky blurts out, "Who the hell is that?" She clicks to look at the other side of the check. "Well he lives in Eugene, Oregon." They asked Mary Hall if there is any way that they can find an address or company for this organization. "Well don't you know, you did donate all of that money to them." Becky is exasperated, "I swear I don't remember coming in here." I have to get a hold of this guy." Mary tells her, "Well I don't know what's going on here but you could try the internet. They made copies of everything, thanked her and left.

They decide to go to the police. After they tell their story to the officer he asks, "So, you recognized yourself on the video?" Becky is so frustrated. "Well, yeah, sort of." He asks, "Is that yes or no?" "It looks like me, but I don't remember being there." Then he asks, "Did your prints match when they checked them while you were withdrawing the money?" "That's what they said." "Then he says, "You think someone planted tiny cameras in your house and a box that is making you eat too much? Are you being told to eat right now?" Becky says irritably, "No, just in my house. He says, "I don't know what to tell you except maybe you should get a hold of a good psychiatrist and maybe if you talk to this Dr. Frond about the money you accidently donated, maybe he'll give it back.

They did a search and found only one in Eugene, Oregon. He is a scientist and has published articles in some science magazines. He has even written a book on subliminal brainwashing." His subjects are of the mind control type. Becky shook her head and said, "Wow" "Do you think that the equipment that was installed in my house was brainwashing me?" He has been retired for a few years. Before that he worked at a psychiatric hospital for the criminally ill. They found an address and phone number in the Eugene, Oregon phone book. Sarah said, "What do you think, do we go there?"

Becky's reply is "Do you think I'll need two seats?" They call and make reservations and discovered that they can get on a flight in three hours. Becky gets Sarah to take Critter, Spike, Oscar and Joey to the vet clinic to stay until they could figure this all out. Then Sarah goes by her house and packs a small overnight bag and Becky does the same thing. She grabs her laptop just in case. The flight only takes a couple of hours. After they landed they rent a car and find a motel close to the airport. The next morning they go in search of Dr. Jacob Frond. They find his mansion without too much trouble and park across the street. As they look on Becky says, "Now what?"

Dr. Frond decides, "I have to calm down. They are just a couple of little girls. Well, a little girl and a big girl. I will have to remove these obstacles from the program. The work is too important. The money is fair payment. With this device I can save our country from terrorism as well as the many other uses that are possible. I can't let this screw it up." "But what?" "I think they may have a bad accident." He decides he needs to keep doing his everyday things so no one becomes suspicious. He maneuvers the monitors to make the blank screen show a recording of past movements of the subject. He makes sure to make it where it will keep playing until he can get back. He calls his assistant Alvin, who is at home and asks him to come in to watch the monitors and continue the brain feeds. He tells him that they are pausing the feeds for the subject Ms. P. He tells him to call if anything unusual happens. He makes arrangements from his home lab while waiting for him to arrive, and then he straightens his tie, grabs his briefcase and leaves his home to go to his office. The government put him an office in the back of a medical supplies company. That is where he types up all of his reports and, where all of the files are kept. He only spends a small amount of time there. He would rather be at home where the monitors are, but he has to go in. When he pulls out of his drive he doesn't notice the car following him.

Becky and Sarah had been sitting outside of Dr. Frond's mansion for about an hour and half when the driveway gate opened. A black Cadillac with tinted windows pulls out and turns onto the street. They can't see inside. They pull out and follow him. Thank goodness they were facing the right direction. They go several blocks and get onto a highway. Then they travel another five miles or so and exit into a business area. Becky and Sarah try to stay back but they don't want to lose him. They go just about a mile and the Cadillac pulls into the parking lot of a nice looking one story brick building with large mirrored windows. There is a sign in front that reads Medical Supplies Unlimited. It then pulls around the side to another parking area. There are a few cars parked in front so they pull in there so they can blend in more. They look at each other and Becky says "We can go in and tell them that we are looking for a motorized scooter for me." Sarah said, "Sounds good." They get out and go in.

When they walk in the door it jingles. They see all kinds of medical supplies such as walkers, walk in baths, oxygen machines, and there is a large counter in the back. A nicely dressed woman is behind the counter. As they walk up she says, "Hello, ladies. My name is Anne. How can I help you today?" Sarah says, "We're looking for a scooter for my sister." The woman shows them the scooters that are available through their store. She turns out to be a chatty lady. All of the time they are discreetly asking questions such as "This is a pretty big building, are there many people working here?" "Yeah, a few." "We noticed a shiny new Cadillac pulling in when we arrived, there must be some very influential people working here." "Oh, that was Dr. Frond. He works in the back. I don't know what he does here. He stays in the back half of the building. He has an office back there. He doesn't mix with us little people. Listen to me; boy did you get me to talking." Becky says, "I love it when people talk. It's a lot better than a quiet person where you have to carry the whole conversation". "How late are you open?" "We stay open until five. Old mister goody two shoes back there usually arrives at ten and leaves at two or three. Wouldn't that be nice?" Becky asks, "Do you have a ladies room that I can use?" Anne says, "Sure, you just go through that door over there, down the hall, last door on the right." Becky looks at Sarah and says, "I'll be right back." While Sarah keeps Anne busy talking in front, Becky decided to check out the back. She goes down the hall and passes the restroom; at the very end of the hall is another door. She goes through it like she is a customer who has lost her way, hoping that Dr. Frond isn't on the other side. He's not. There is a warehouse area with all kinds of crates and medical supplies stored on shelves. She walks further in and goes down one of aisles between the shelves. She walks to the end. The area isn't very big but she is getting out of breath. At the end she sees another door in the very back. There are shelves lining the back wall too. She's feeling tired too. She checks the door and finds it is unlocked so she eases it open just a crack and peeks in. there is a hallway running horizontal to the shelving in the warehouse. There is a door with a name plate on it directly across from the door into the warehouse. It reads Dr. Jacob Frond. She looks at the lock on the door and sees that it isn't a big heavy duty one. She has to get back to the store area before Anne gets suspicious. She hurries back as fast as she can at her size. When she goes through the door back into the store she is really out of breath. She makes her way over to Sarah and Anne. Sarah asks, "Are you alright?" "Just a little tired. Could we come back tomorrow, I'm not feeling well? Sarah says, "Sure, would that be ok with you Anne?" "That will be fine; I'll find you one of our catalogues." She hurries around the counter and comes back around holding the catalogue. She hands it to Becky and says, "I'll see you tomorrow then. You ladies have a nice evening." Sarah takes Becky's arm and they leave. When they get out to the car Sarah asks, "Are you really alright?" Becky says "Yeah, this weight is a lot to carry around though." They go back to their motel room to discuss their next move.

They stop to get something to eat on their way back. They sit at the table in their room and talk while they eat. Becky tells her the layout of the back area of the store and about the office door. She says, "It's probably locked when he's out. We need to find a way to get in there." Sarah says, "Is it just a regular door lock, or is there a dead bolt?" Becky thought for a second and said, "I believe it's just a regular door lock, they probably have a security system that is set when the store is closed." Sarah looks sort of funny for a second and says, "I hope this doesn't make you think less of me, but I know how to pick locks." Becky opens her eyes wide in surprise and asks, "What! You're kidding. I would never have guessed. You are so clean cut. Where in the world did you learn how to pick locks? She shakes her head and says, "Will the wonders ever cease?" Sarah just laughs and tells her about a boyfriend that she had when she was in her late teens that would burglarize businesses. One night they were partying together and he showed her how to pick a lock. "It's not hard, here watch." She stood up and pulled a bobby pin out of her hair and went to the bathroom door. "We'll have to use this door because of the card thing on the other one." She locks the door and using the bobby pin she unlocks it. Becky says, "Ok, then." and laughs. They decide to go back in the morning before ten and this time Becky will distract the counter woman Anne and Sarah will go back to Dr. Frond's office and do a quick search.

They get up the next morning feeling nervous, but determined. They go to a hardware store and buy a couple of screwdrivers just in case and put them in Sarah's purse. Then they head to the medical supply store.

When they arrive at the medical supply store they pull around back first to see if the black Cadillac is there. It isn't so they pulled around to the store side. There is another car parked right in front there so they take their time going in. They enter the store to the jingle of the bell and walk around casually looking. When Anne finishes helping the older couple that are looking at wheelchairs she comes over and says, "Good morning ladies how are you today?" Becky says "Oh, we're good. We looked at the catalogue, but in all honestly I would like to look at that one over there."She points to a scooter that is on the show floor. I didn't get to look around much yesterday like I would have liked to, you know because I was feeling bad and all." Anne asks, "Oh yeah, how are you feeling today, better I hope?" Becky replies, "Yes, much better, thank you." Sarah asks "Could I use your restroom please?" Anne tells her "Sure, down the hall last door on the right." Sarah leaves Becky to look at scooters and makes her way back to Dr. Frond's office. She goes the way Becky had told her and finds his office easily. She removes a bobby pin from her hair and picks the lock quickly thinking "Like an old pro" His office has a desk, filing cabinet, and a lighted fish aquarium. She shuts the door quietly, turns the light on and looks around. She walks over to his desk first. It is very organized. She opens the drawer in front and sees pens and paperclips and such. She then opens the drawer on the right side and there is a stapler, post-its and other miscellaneous stuff. There's a calendar on his desk. She looks at it and sees notes on different dates for meetings and appointments. Everything in his office is very impersonal, too organized except that on the fifth day of the month she sees a smiley face and "ONE DOWN" She thinks, "I wonder what that means." She opens the bigger drawer on the right side and inside there are some books and a folder. On the tab of the folder is B. Peterson. She grabs it up and stuffs it halfway in the front of her pants and pulls her shirt down over it. "She needs to hurry." She goes over to the filing cabinet and great, it's locked. She goes back over to the desk and has an idea. She pulls the front drawer open again and reaches deep in the back and woo hoo it's there. She's bad about putting her file cabinet key in the same place, not after this though. She pulls the small key out and rushes over to the file cabinet and it fits. She opens it and inside are more files like the one she already has. It looks like about twenty of them. She thinks "Will they fit?" Thank goodness she wore loose fitting slacks and a jacket. She stuffs all of the files into her pants, shuts the file drawer and rushes out the door, locking it behind her. She made it through the door into the warehouse and jogs across to the other door. She peeks out, then slips through back into the hallway. She has her shirt pulled over the bulking folders and her jacket pulled closed with her purse in front of her when Anne sticks her head through the door at the other end of the hall. "Oh, there you are, we were beginning to worry."

Sarah says, "Oh I'm sorry. I didn't mean to worry you two. It's my stomach." She said this making the "you know" face. She sort of hunches forward trying not to look suspicious and went through the door and straight to Becky and says, "I'm afraid we need to leave immediately, I'm so sick to my stomach." She sort of does a retching thing for Anne's benefit. Anne says, "Yes, by all means, we can do this another time." Becky is fighting back laughter as they rushed out of the door. They get out of there as fast as they can.

Dr. Frond is on a plane to Dallas. He needs to figure out what kind of accident he should help them have. Maybe a car accident. He arrives in Dallas and goes immediately to Becky's house. Her garage door is closed so he doesn't really know whether she is home or not. It's still early, he'll wait. He stays there for three hours and nothing happens. Where could she be? She's too big to do too much. Maybe she's at Sarah's house. He has her address and he puts it into his GPS. When he gets to her house it's the same thing "No movement." He stays there for a couple of hours and decides to leave. He goes to a hotel that isn't too far from Becky's house. He decides to go back later in the evening and stay. This may take a little longer than he had expected.

Becky and Sarah get back to their room and spread the folders out on the bed. They start reading them and can't believe it. After awhile Becky says, "We're all guinea pigs. And he's robbing us too!" They put the files in stacks depending on where they live. In each stack there are five folders. There is Dallas, New York, Los Angeles, and Miami. Becky is looking at the Dallas files. In this stack is her file, Patti Dawson, Charlie Crouse, Julie Wong and Zack James. In all there are twenty. In each file there are addresses, occupations, background information, health information, weekly reports, behaviors, daily habits. Becky starts crying and says, "I am so mad I want to go find him and kill him. He has been watching me for over seven months. Oh my God. How embarrassing." Sarah hugs Becky and tells her, "We'll get him, we can't kill him but we'll make sure he is locked up forever." Sarah picks up the Zack

James file and says "Look here, I wonder what this means." On the front of this one the word "Departed" is scrawled in ink. She opens it up and looks through it. Everything looks the same as the others except on the last page of the reports at the bottom written larger than the other print are the words "The End". She glances up and spots the word suicide and reads some. "Oh, wow this guy killed himself." "This is horrible." Becky looks pale. She says, "We need to go back to Dallas and find this Patti Dawson, Charlie Crouse and Julie Wong. There's strength in numbers. Then we can go to the police again." They called to find a flight back and were told that they could leave late that evening. They go through the files and write down everyone's addresses and phone numbers. Before their flight they already have all the information they need to find the Dallas group.

They arrive in Dallas at two in the morning and call a cab to take them to Becky's house. When they get inside Becky says, "You know, we can't stay here. He's probably looking for us. We need to get the box of equipment and I need more clothes and then we need to get out of here as fast as we can." Sarah says, "Your right, he already tried to run me down." "Let's get out of here; he may already be in Dallas." Becky gathers what she will need to be gone for a couple of days and Sarah picks up the box of equipment and they go through the kitchen and out of the door leading into the garage. Becky's car is parked there. They put everything in the trunk and get in. She opens the garage door and they leave, looking all around as they go. Nothing suspicious. They don't see the black Cadillac parked a block away in the driveway of an empty house. It is mostly hidden by a bush beside the driveway at the house.

Dr. Frond watches as the taxi leaves the women at Becky's house. He is wondering what they were up to. He sat there for about a half hour trying to decide what to do when the garage door opens and Becky's blue Mercedes pulls out. He is parked a block away in a driveway of a house that's empty and he has a good view of her house. They head towards town and he follows them. There isn't any good place to run them off of the road. This area doesn't have any cliffs or bridges. Damn it, I'm going to have to shoot them. He had stopped by his acquaintance house on the way for another gun. I wanted this to look like an accident. Well, it can't be helped. About that time the Mercedes speeds up. He's been spotted.

They hadn't gone far when Becky noticed the car that is following them. "We're being followed" she says. Sarah looks back and sees the headlights of several cars and asks "How do you know? There are several cars behind us." Becky tells her that the second car, a black Toyota has been behind them since they left her house. She speeds up and weaves through traffic and then turns down a street and makes the block and gets back on the same street. The black car follows. Becky tells Sarah, "We can't go to your house. I'm going to try to lose him." She really speeds up then. She puts some space between them and turns down a side street, and then she turns down an alley that cuts through. The alley comes out on another street that takes them back to the street that they started on. They get back on the same street going in the opposite direction. They lose him. They decide to go out by the interstate where all of the motels are and rent a room. They're pretty shook up and it's five o'clock in the morning so they sleep awhile and when they wake at noon they start out calling Patti Dawson.

Becky calls Patti Dawson and leaves a message on her phone. "Ms. Dawson, you don't know me, but my name is Dr. Becky Peterson and I know what you are going through. I have some information you may be interested in. Please meet me at the coffee shop across the street from your apartment. I know this is a lot to ask but it's important. Let's say two o'clock." "Please, this is really important." Becky knows from experience that they won't answer their phones. She was avoiding people before Sarah got to her. They then called Charlie Crouse and Julie Wong and left messages of the same sort leaving time gaps that allowed for travel and time spent with each. They had to arrange to meet at their homes because of the locations. Hopefully they will open their doors.

Charlie Crouse can't help but look in the mirror as he passes. He used to look so different. Charlie is the owner of a line of hunting clubs located in Colorado, Iowa, and Louisiana. He is known to have the best survivalist skills by all who have known him and a lot of people know him. His clubs are the most luxurious and offer more hunting opportunities than any other. Before he had gained the three hundred pounds he was in better health than anyone that he knows. He doesn't know what happened but about eight months ago he started eating uncontrollably. He was standing there looking at himself with his stained up t-shirt and sweat pants, a piece of chicken in one hand. All he does now is eat and sleep. He has shut himself off from all of his friends. About then his phone rings. He doesn't answer it any more; he lets the answering machine get it. When the message gives the beep a woman's voice says, "Mr. Crouse you don't know who I am but we have something in common. About eight months ago I started eating and couldn't stop. Before this I was a healthy person. I know what is causing this change. I would like to come to your house so we can talk. I will be there in two hours. Please let me in." "Oh yeah, my name is Dr. Becky Peterson."

Patti cannot resist going to the coffee shop at two. When she walks in she is immediately recognized by Becky and Sarah because of her size. She sees two women standing at the counter waving at her. One is a slim brunette and the other is a very overweight blonde. She walks over and they ask, "Are you Patti Dawson?" She leans on the counter huffing and puffing and says, "Yes, what's going on?" They tell her that there is a cement bench outside that they could go out and sit on. The furniture in the coffee shop is rather fragile looking. She agrees and they walk out to the bench and both of the larger ladies sit down. Sarah doesn't say anything but she worries about the bench holding. They tell Patti what they have found out and hand her the folder with her name on it. She sits and reads. She flips through the reports that are actually a daily log of her activities. She starts crying and says, "I knew that something was happening but I didn't know what. I bet they

53

installed the equipment when I had my internet worked on. It's been about eight months ago, about the time my eating started. Oh my God! I can't believe this. I wonder if he is responsible for Mia." "She told them about Mia's murder. I can't go back in there." Becky says, "I don't think you should go back into your apartment." Sarah goes in and gets them all some coffee and they discuss their next move. Patti had brought her purse so she didn't have to go back in her apartment. She was holding a bag of candy and she put it in her purse. All of a sudden she wasn't as hungry as usual. They decided to take Becky's Mercedes and find a place to rent a van. They figure they would be picking up more weight and didn't think that her car could handle much more. They take Patti to her bank and were told about the same thing that Becky was told. They head over to Charlie Crouse's house.

Charlie lives down a long tree lined drive. His house is a huge rustic log cabin with a wraparound porch. His yard is well kept with flower beds and fountains that flow into beautiful pools. Off to one side is a large vegetable garden. The place is beautiful. They walk up onto his porch where there is a porch swing and comfortable looking chairs and plants everywhere. They ring his doorbell and wait. After a couple of minutes they hear footsteps. This guy sounds pretty big. They are feeling nervous. "How is this guy going to react?" When he opens the door there stands a really large man. He has blond curly hair and hazel eyes that have a kindness to them. He is also holding a sandwich. He says, "Good evening ladies, your call took me completely by surprise and made me so curious that I could hardly stand it." "Becky started with, "Mr. Crouse have you been eating uncontrollably, almost compulsively? "Are you usually a very health conscious person?" "Do you feel like you can't control yourself?" Charlie Crouse just stands there shaking his head yes. Then he says, "First, call me Charlie, second how do you know this?" Becky looks at the chairs on his porch and sees that they look sturdy. "Would you mind?" He says, "No, of course, please ladies would you like to sit?" They all sit and Becky starts out, but they all tell Charlie all that they know so far and show him the files that they had taken from Dr. Frond's office. His file is on top and they hand him that one. He sits there in front of them and reads. He reads some of the personal information in front and then he looks through the rest. When he gets to the pages that are the reports, he reads some more. When he looks up after he is done the look on his face expresses anger and shock. He says, "What the hell is this?"

Becky asks "Did you have something installed in your house about eight months ago?" He says, "I had a security system installed." Becky tells him, "The way it looks is that we have all been brainwashed. We need this confirmed but as soon as Patti and I got away from our homes we stopped eating. "Well, we took all of the equipment out of my house" Becky says, "so he knows that I know. He killed Patti's friend and he tried to run Sarah down with a car so we are all in danger." He has also been taking our money and we have no memory of taking money out of our accounts and sending it to him." "He may be taking your money too." He stands up and starts to go into his house but they stop him. "If you go in he will have control again." He stops and turns around. "What can we do?" Becky says, "We don't know, we're trying to figure it all out." He goes over to one of the chairs and sits down. They are all quiet. Charlie is trying to grasp what is happening. He says, "Ok, I have a friend. She used to be a cop, now she's a private detective. I can call her. She has connections that may help." "I have to get my wallet out of the house and then I will go with you." He struggles up out of the chair and walks over to the door. He stands there a minute and then opens the door and enters. He is only inside for a couple of minutes and he comes out stuffing a pistol in the pocket of a sweat jacket. Becky says, "We need to go to Julie Wong's house and then we can go back to the motel and call your friend."

"Where did they go?"Dr. Frond is at a loss. He hadn't figured that they would spot him. That's the disadvantage of using such accomplished subjects. He waited for a while at Sarah's house. Nothing. He decides all that he can do for now is go back to his room and try to come up with a plan. He thinks hard. Where would they go? "Of course the cashier's check." If Becky isn't under hypnosis anymore then she may know about the money. She could have found out my name and address. Could she be in Oregon? He calls his assistant Alvin and asks if anything has changed. He says only that Patti Dawson left her apartment and has been gone for a long time and that Charlie Crouse has left his house too. That would be unusual because neither one of them have left their homes in five months at least. He tells him. I need you to leave the monitors for about an hour and run to my office at the medical supply store. There is an extra key taped to the bottom of the key board in front of the monitors. When you get inside my office look around to see if you notice anything out of place. Call me from there. Dr. Frond hung up and waited.

Julie Wong is a very accomplished doctor of neurology. She has a private practice and she works at a major hospital in the Dallas area though she hasn't worked in awhile. Julie also volunteers as Binky the clown and entertains the children on the pediatric oncology floor at the hospital. She hasn't done that in a while either. Her parents moved to the United States from China a couple of years before she was born. Her parents made sure that she went to school and had every opportunity that America had to offer. Her parents went to live back in China after she was grown though. They are very traditional. Julie's house is decorated in a mixture of American and Chinese. She has her low table with cushions for meals and there are mats and she removes her shoes before entering. She had been eating in the kitchen lately because she has gained so much weight that she can't get up and down good enough to eat at her table. No matter what she does she can't stop eating. She has always lived a very healthy life except for the last eight months or so. She weighs almost three hundred pounds and hasn't left her house in the last five months or so. She doesn't answer her phone any more unless it is her parents. She hasn't told them about her weight gain because they would be very disappointed. If she doesn't talk to them they will come to America and check on her.

When they arrived at Julie Wong's house they decide it would be best if only Becky and Sarah go to the door. They didn't want to scare her. She lives in a nice brick house in a really nice neighborhood. They walk up onto her porch and they ring her doorbell and wait. Nothing happens. Becky says, "She probably thinks I'm crazy and won't answer." They ring the bell again, still nothing. They go back to the van and get in. Becky tells the others, "She won't answer. What can we do?" Patti hands her a cell phone and says, "Call her. I know that she won't pick up but try and talk her into opening the door." Becky calls and when the beep comes she says, "Dr. Wong, I know that you are worried about talking to us, but there is something going on that you need to know about. It means life or death. Please answer the door. I promise you I am sane. The woman with me is my friend Sarah and she's sane too." "We are here to help you." "Sarah and I are going to walk up to your door and ring your bell again. Please talk to us." They walk back up to the door and ring the bell. This time she opens the door. She is a large oriental woman wearing a bright flowered silk caftan. She has a very suspicious look on her face as she asks, "What do you want?" She is holding a bag of cookies in one hand and is chewing. Becky says, "Could you please step out here so we can talk to you?" Julie Wong says, "I don't think I need to do that." Sarah pleads, "Please, Doctor it's so important. You will understand after you hear what we need to tell you. I have something to show you too." "Please." She opens the door and comes out onto her porch. "Ok, what is it?" Becky says, "Let's sit down." motioning toward the steps. The lawn furniture on her porch doesn't look very sturdy. She says, "I sit there, I may not get up." Exasperated Becky says, "Ok, but if you feel faint or anything just sit straight down. Ok?" Dr. Wong says, "Ok, already, so tell me what is so important!" Becky is getting so frustrated. She says, "Dr. Wong, have you felt that you have lost control of your eating?" She hands her the file with her name on it. Julie Wong reads the information in the front. She flips through the rest scanning everything. She looks up with tears in her eyes and starts yelling, "Where did you get this? Tell me now. I'm going to call the police." Becky says, "Hold on Dr. let me explain, we tried going to the police and they didn't take us seriously. Let me tell you the whole story." Becky and Sarah tell her everything they know so far. She does sit on the steps then. She tells her about the others in the van and asks if she can get them to come talk to her too. She agrees and they motion for the others to come. Here comes a big blond curly haired man and a big brunette lumbering up her sidewalk. It's too crazy to not be true. They all stand and talk a little longer. Dr. Wong finally relaxes some and tells them to call her Julie. She agrees to go with them.

When they get to the motel the others rent rooms too. None of them want to go back to their homes. Charlie and Julie checked their bank balances and both discover large amounts of money missing. They all meet in Becky and Sarah's room and they talk about what they need to do next. Charlie says, "I've called my friend Jeana Garcia and she has agreed to help us. She will be here in an hour. Becky says, "Well that's a start. Anymore ideas?" "Julie replies, "Maybe we can confront him." Sarah says, "He's dangerous, he tried to kill me and he murdered Patti's friend Mia." Julie says, "I am so angry I feel like I can kill him with my bare hands." Patti says, "We need to work together and what about all of the other people that he's doing this to." Julie asks, "Why can't we go to the police?" Becky says, "We tried that and they wouldn't take us seriously. We were told that we needed to talk to a psychiatrist." This went on until there was a knock at the door and Jeana Garcia arrived. She is a small Hispanic woman. When she enters the room she can't help but look surprised. She looks over at Charlie and says, "Lord have mercy, is that you Charlie?" She reached out and grabbed his extended hand and shook it vigorously. "Como estas, you loco ole gringo?" Charlie says, "I've been better Jeana. I've got some really crazy stuff happening here." He leads her to one of the chairs in the room and gets her all settled to hear their story. Charlie starts talking. Off and on during the story Jeana would ask a question and either him or one of the others would answer. When he is done she sits quietly for a few minutes thinking. Everyone is quiet. She says, "Ok, we have to find this guy. Where would he be? He knows that Becky and Sarah know

58

about the devices. He probably knows about the rest of you now too." Charlie says, "There are other victims. You need to look at the folders." Sarah takes them out of one of the dresser drawers. Jeana spreads them out on the table and goes through them.

Dr. Frond is so deep in thought that he jumps when the phone rings. It's his assistant Alvin. "I'm in your office now and everything looks normal." Dr. Frond tells him, "Open the drawer on the bottom right side of the desk and tell me if you see a file in there with the name B. Peterson on it." Alvin says, "There isn't a file in here." Dr. Frond is stunned. "It can't be gone. Are you sure?" Yes, Dr. Frond, there is no file in here." Dr. Frond says, "Ok, I want you to open the drawer on top in front and reach to the very back and there should be a key." "Is it there?" Alvin says, "It's not here." Dr. Frond is thinking "Can it get any worse?" Alvin, I need you to check the file cabinet and see if it's locked. After a minute he hears "It's unlocked and it's empty." Dr. Frond says, "Alvin, I want you to go back to the monitors and watch closely and inform me of anything the least bit out of kilter. I'm going to head that way."

After a while Jeana looks up and says, "I have a plan." We have three remaining cities with five people in each city. We can split up and inform and recruit. We will all gather with the devices, files and the subjects when we're done and then we will talk to the F.B.I. Ok we have Becky, Patti, Julie and Charlie. Then there is me and Sarah. That's six. That means two to a city. Let's team up. Becky says, "Sarah and I have already been working on this for a while, and besides she picks locks." "Sarah says, "Hey, you don't have to tell everybody about that." Jeana says, "Ok, that's one. Patti says, "So, Dr. Julie what do you think? Julie says, "Sounds great, just two big girls out for a good time." They both laugh and high five. Charlie looks at Jeana and says, "I guess it's you and me." "Now, who wants what city?" Julie says, "I've been to New York before." Patti shakes her head and says "That sounds good to me." Charlie whispers to Jeana and she shakes her head yes and says, "We'll take Los Angeles." Becky says, "Ok, me and Sarah will take Miami. They all start making flight reservations and exchanging cell phone numbers. They looked in the files to get the addresses and phone numbers for each one. Everybody is able to get on a flight at different times in the morning. That evening they all go out to dinner together. They laugh and talk about the poor employees when they saw them come through the door. Everyone ate lighter than they had in a long time. Becky went back to her vegetarian diet. They all talked about their lives before all of this and they laughed about Becky being a vegetarian veterinarian.

The next morning they were all a little nervous but they boarded their flights and flew to the cities that they had decided on. They had the files for the people that they needed to talk to. They also had their addresses and phone numbers. It took each team a week to talk to, remove devices and get their group of subjects on a plane to Dallas. Most of them had to buy two seats to travel. They found rooms for everyone in the same hotel. People automatically thought they were with some kind of convention. As fast as they talked them into going they got them on a plane. At the end of the week they gathered at the rented convention area in the hotel. Jeana Garcia invited the Federal Bureau of Investigations to listen to what has been going on. They weren't sure about the methods that were used to get the files but it was a case of life or death. They decided to pick Dr. Jacob Frond up. They arranged for a swat team to swarm his mansion and some were disbanded to search his office. When they didn't find him in either place they sent agents to all of the airports, train stations and border stops. They caught him trying to cross the border to Mexico. He had a satchel full of money with him when he was picked up. The government denied having anything to do with Dr. Frond's work.

All of the subjects of the study went into drastic weight loss programs and most had plastic surgery to repair the damage done by their weight gain. They all recovered their money that was stolen and kept in touch. Dr. Frond was charged with twenty counts of aggravated assault with a deadly weapon, twenty counts of fraud, one count of murder, and an attempted murder. He was sentenced to twenty life sentences.

THE END

MONSTER ON LOVELY LANE

Life is not that your heart beats, that you breathe, that you can walk around.

Your life is what surrounds you. What makes you happy. Like love, beauty and joy.

You took that from me. So you took my life. Now I must take yours.

The day is warm, with the wind blowing softly. The sun is bright and the sky is cloudless and blue. There is a pond with lily pads at the edges and ducks gliding across the middle. On the grass beside the pond, a woman and a man have laid a blanket on the ground and have put all kinds of delicious looking food on it. There are a little boy and girl playing with a dog a short distance away. They are throwing a ball back and forth between them and trying to keep it away from the dog. I had been sitting on this bench for an hour or two, I'm not sure and all I can think is "What happened". That used to be my life. It seems like a hundred years ago.

My name is David Jones. I had been married sixteen years to my beautiful wife Kate. We had two kids. Kelly five and Danny seven. Kate and I met while in the army. She was my firecracker. I fell in love the first time I ever saw her. She was jogging around in fatigues carrying a gun. I thought she was perfect. We had a great home. A lot of the time loud and hectic, I loved it.

I was working at my job as a property manager at Home Sweet Home Management Company "The property management people that will find the right home for the right family every time". When my next appointment arrived, the receptionist buzzed me. "Mr. and Mrs. Grant are here." I told her to send them in. They entered my office and were a nice looking

63

couple in their thirties I would guess. I had talked to Mr. Grant several times on the phone. We had agreed to meet, so I could show them a couple of houses. They were relocating from Las Vegas, Nevada to the Dallas area and were looking for a house. Mr. Grant said that they were in need of a three or four bedroom home in a good neighborhood with good schools. He had told me that he was going to be managing a new construction company opening in our area. Mr. Grant is a large man; he has dark hair and is tanned from the sun. His wife has beautiful blonde hair, perfect features and figure. Mr. Grant had informed me in our phone calls that she is a music teacher and would like to have a place to give piano lessons in their new home. So a den or office in the house would be necessary. I greeted the two, "Hello there Mr. and Mrs. Grant, it is so nice to finally meet you. How are you doing today?" Mr. Grant replied, "Oh, we are doing great. We haven't had a chance to look around much, but from what we have seen so far it's beautiful here. "I'm George and this is Andrea. Our son Jason and our daughter Emily had to stay with their Grandmother because of school". Andrea just smiled in agreement. They seemed like the perfect family.

I had three houses to show them that day that were in their price range. We took my SUV, plenty of room, and went to look at an older two story wood frame house first. The address, a little unusual, is 1313 Lovely Lane. I felt like this was the perfect house for them. It has three bedrooms, two baths, a nice big porch, and a den. In the back yard, there is a tire swing hanging from a huge old oak tree. There used to be a well. It was cemented over years ago. The property is bordered by large pine trees and it is located on the outskirts of the city. We went and looked at the other two, just perfunctionary really because I already knew that the first one was it. When they saw this place, they knew it was the one too. We negotiated the lease a week later and they were ready to move in a month after that.

I went home that evening with a bottle of wine because I had made a really good commission on this deal. This house hadn't been the easiest to lease because of that old well. The top had been sealed off with concrete, but it had deteriorated quite a bit and the owner just wouldn't have it repaired. Mr. and Mrs. Grant hadn't said anything about it and I hadn't mentioned it either. So deal done. I walked into my house that evening and was struck with wonderful food smells coming from the kitchen. The TV was on in the living room even though no one was watching it. I walked over and turned it off. I heard Danny playing video games in the other room. I walked into the kitchen and Kelly was sitting at the table coloring in one of her coloring books. Kate was at the sink washing lettuce for a salad. She turned around and I was stunned by how beautiful she is. I gave her a big hello kiss and said, "something smells good in here." I walked over and gave Kelly a kiss on top of her head and said, "I finally leased that Lovely Lane house that has been a pain in my butt forever." Kelly said, "Daddddddddy, the language please. Little ears here." I put the wine on the counter and tripped over Rufus. He was our lab, german shepherd mix. He had been with us for about four years and for some reason, he was always where I was walking. I said "Oh, sorry princess little ears." About that time Danny walked in, I ruffled his hair as he said "I'm hungry." Kate replied, "five minutes, you two go wash up." "You too dad." We had supper in the dining room. We were all laughing and joking. It was a celebration for my deal that day. After supper the kids took their baths and went to bed. Kate and I sat out on our porch with glasses of wine and talked and enjoyed our private time together. It seems like it was only yesterday.

Moving day George pulled up in his ford explorer. Jason had ridden with him. Andrea was behind them in her car with Emily. Jason looks just like his father and Emily looks like her mother. They all jumped out happily. The kids ran around the yard excitedly. George and Andrea met in the middle and put their arms around each other's waist as they looked at their new Texas home. George said, "I wonder where the moving van is." And then they walked up to the house. When they reached the front door they turned around and yelled, "Kids come on, let's look inside." Jason and Emily ran up to them, Emily put her arm comfortably around George's waist and said "I love you daddy." George said, "You too Punkin". Andrea grabbed Jason and pulled him to her. They unlocked the door and went in. When they were inside the front door they could see the gleaming wood floors and a large rock fireplace. There is a staircase to the left that goes up to the bedrooms and the one bath that is up there. There is a den to the left right before the stairs and a door across the living room directly in front of the front door. Through that door is the kitchen, laundry and a second bathroom. There are these old fashion saloon type swinging doors hanging there. The kids took off running again, trying to look everywhere at once. George and Andrea just laughed and hugged each other. About that time they heard the moving truck pull into the driveway. Things became really busy then. They decided that the den would make a perfect music room for Andrea to do her piano lessons. They moved her piano in there and she hung all of her paintings of instruments on the walls.

That evening they sat on the front porch with glasses of wine. George said, "It's like this house was made for us." They talked into the night, about how wonderful life is going to be in their new house. Then they stumbled upstairs, made love and happily passed out. They spent the rest of the weekend getting settled in. Monday morning George would start his new job.

Monday morning George arrived at a big metal shop with a couple of leans about twenty minutes from his house. There is already a sign up. It reads 'Diamond in the Rough Builders Inc.' Other than that the place is pretty bare. George sees a red pickup with a toolbox, ladder rack with ladder, and other assorted tools in the back. This must be Mr. Redman. George was told that Redman or Red is what he is called had been a carpenter for about thirty years and would be over five crews that would build houses and other structures all over the Arklatex. There is also a blue Mazda. Probably Jack Cooper, the sales representative. They all got together and Jack told him about the jobs that are already being arranged. They need to set up communications, and order materials. They also need a forklift and tools. They have work trucks being brought over tomorrow. Red interviews laborers and leads. George has to meet with the new bookkeeper at three. Everything is coming together great.

Meanwhile Andrea is getting the kids into school, stocking the house with groceries, getting her advertising out for piano lessons. Pretty much gathering what she needs to put their home together. Everything is going great. She found the school to her liking. The teachers seemed very nice. She even met a couple of the other parents that were interested in having their kids take piano lessons. She went by the florist and picked up some flowers. This is going to be a wonderful evening. She looks at the time and realizes she isn't going to make it home in time to meet the kids when they get off the bus. She is only going to be about ten minutes late at most. She tries to hurry; the car in front of her is going so slow. She can't get around; it's a two lane road. Traffic is heavy. George is twenty minutes away. Damn it, damn it, damn it!

The bus driver is really pleased; she is doing her route in good time today. She pulls up to the new kid's house, it looks quiet, but from her understanding the mother works at home. Jason and Emily get off of the bus. They walk into their yard and turn and wave. The bus drives away. They begin walking up to the house and Jason says "I wonder where Mamas' car is." When they get to the front door, it's locked. "She must be running late. Let's just play out here until she gets home." They take off around the house; they figure they will hear her when she pulls up.

Jason is chasing Emily around pretending to be a monster. He is growling and has his arms up and his fingers are splayed like claws. Emily is giggling and running around. As she runs across the top of the sealed well it creaks, but she doesn't notice. She makes a circle and when she reaches the well again the top gives and she falls through. There is a short scream, more like a squeak than a scream. Jason runs over screaming himself and looks down into the well. It's deep and dark. He sees her pale form at the bottom. He hears his Mama pull into the driveway and he runs around the house crying hysterically. When Andrea sees him she jumps out of the car and runs to him, "what's wrong, where's Emily." All he can do is cry and point and say she fell in the hole. Andrea runs around the house, she sees where the hole is. She runs over calling "Emily! Emily! Are you ok. Emily!" She reaches the well and looks in. She can vaguely make out some broken cement pieces at the bottom, and there is Emily. She looks like a broken doll.

She calls nine, one, one, and George. George rushes home. He doesn't even remember the trip later. Emily did not survive the fall. All George could think is, why hadn't I noticed this old well before. Why hadn't they warned us about it? I have been too tied up in everything to even think about my family's safety. Andrea just could not be consoled. She cried as if she was in physical and emotional agony. The EMT's called a local doctor to come to the house and he gave her some sedatives. George went into autopilot. He called Andrea's mother and from there the family showed up to take care of them. A numb fog. That is the best way to describe how George was. Andrea lay on their bed like a zombie. She doesn't talk. It is like she is catatonic. Andrea's mother Janice takes care of her and Jason. Jason just cries and cries. And then he shuts down too.

It was determined a tragic accident. The funeral was the next Saturday. Janice offered to take Jason home with her after the funeral so George and Andrea could get themselves together. They were both in such deep mourning that they weren't there for Jason. After everyone left, George and Andrea lay on their bed staring at the ceiling. George decided he needed a drink. He asked Andrea if she would be alright for about an hour so he could run to the liquor store. All they ever have in their house is wine and he needs something stronger. She just sort of mutters something that sounds like ok. He goes out and gets in his truck and goes to the liquor store; he is still running on autopilot. He finds his way there and is back in about an hour. He gets this strange feeling when he pulls into the driveway. He goes into the house, right inside the door there is a table. He sets a bottle of vodka down there and goes upstairs to check on Andrea. He looks in the bedroom and she is still on the bed just where she was when he left. She's very still. He walks over and she is so still. He puts his hand on her chest and there is no movement. He just knows. He glances over at the bedside table and sees a glass of water with half of the water gone and the pill bottle with the sedatives in it that the doctor had left for her. He picks up the pill bottle and it is empty. He shakes her over and over and over. "No! No! No! You can't do this!" That is when his mind snaps.

He goes downstairs and pours a big glass of vodka and sits in a chair in the dark and drinks it. He thinks, this is somebody's fault. This is an evil house. Why didn't that guy tell us about the well? This evil house has taken everything away. We were so happy. Why didn't he tell us? He killed my family. I need to find him and kill him. He goes into the music room where there is a desk in one corner. He opens drawers until he finds the lease papers. There is the leasing agent's name, David Jones. There is a phone on the desk and a phone book beside it. He looks up David Jones. His address is 2233 Walker Rd. home phone number 555-1199. He picks up the phone and calls the number. The phone rings three times and then a male voice says hello. George says, "You have taken everything away, now I have nothing" and he hangs up. He throws the phone across the room. He pours himself another glass of vodka and sits back in the chair in the dark. He passes out there.

The Saturday of the funeral David Jones and his family slept late. They had just returned the night before from a vacation in Galveston. It was a wonderful trip. They started moving around about nine o'clock. Kate got up first and started the coffee going. David went out to get the paper. When he comes back in he trips over Rufus and throws the paper on the counter and asks, "How bout I make my famous blueberry pancakes?" Kate says, "That would be wonderful" and gives David a great big kiss. They hadn't heard about Emily. The kids stumble down all rumpled and sleepy looking. Kate says, "Daddy's making blueberry pancakes." Kelly says, "Woo Hoo." Danny says, "Cool." They head into the living room to catch some cartoons. They have a nice family breakfast. While they eat Kate asks, "How about we have a picnic tomorrow? We can go to the park; you know the one with the pond and the ducks.

We can even take Rufus with us." They all agree that it sounds nice.

They all just hang out at home, the kids playing in their rooms or outside. David forgets about the paper and picks up a book that he had been reading on the beach in Galveston. He reads awhile and then watches a movie on TV until he falls asleep on the couch. He wakes up with the kids running through the house. Danny is acting like a monster with his arms in the air and his fingers spread like claws. He is growling and chasing Kelly and she is giggling and dodging around. He yells for them to settle down in the house. He hears Kate in the kitchen and looks at the clock and is surprised to see that it is already after five o'clock. He wonders into the kitchen and sees that Kate is making a meatloaf. She is just putting it in the oven. She has some potatoes in a bowl getting ready to peel them. In about an hour supper is ready and they sit down to eat. They all sit around the table and talk and laugh. After they eat the kids go take their baths and get ready for bed. David helps Kate clean up the supper dishes. While they are cleaning the phone rings and David dries his hands and goes into the living room to answer it. When he picks it up a gravelly sounding voice says, "You have taken everything away, now I have nothing." Then the man hangs up. David is stunned. He tries calling the number back but it just rings and no one answers. They put the kids to bed and sit out on the porch with glasses of wine. David decides he would check into it tomorrow. He didn't want to upset Kate so he didn't tell her about it. They have a quiet somber evening. Just comfortable being together.

The next morning they get up and go to church. It's a nice service. They get home around ten forty five and Kate starts getting their picnic food together. She makes some chicken, potato salad, beans and one of those apple pies that you just pop in the oven for half an hour. She put it all in a basket, and grabbed a blanket to eat on. She put some sodas and bottle water in an ice chest. They all load up. They leave about twelve or so. Rufus is sitting in between Danny and Kelly in the back seat. They get to the park, it is a beautiful day. The sun is shining. There is a nice soft breeze. The kids brought a ball and are throwing it around. Rufus is running around trying to get it. A wonderful day. They don't even notice the scruffy looking man sitting on the bench watching them. David hadn't even thought about the call.

George wakes up at about seven or so and his head is killing him. He stumbles up the stairs and into the bathroom, where he finds aspirin in the medicine cabinet. He uses the bathroom and looks at himself in the mirror and it hits him. What his life has become. He feels total desolation. He has nothing left. He feels rage. Total blinding rage. He goes out into the hall and looks at the door to his bedroom. He goes to the door and pauses. He walks in and sits on the bed next to Andrea. She hasn't moved. He touches her hand, it is cold. He tells her. "I'm going to fix it. I love you Andrea and I'm going to make it right." He goes back downstairs and into the music room, in his mind he sees Andrea playing her piano. She is so beautiful when she plays. George thinks, "How could he do this to me? You took everything I love away, my family, my home, my happiness." He walks over to the desk and looks at the phone book, it's still open. There is his address. He underlines it and then tears the page from the book. He opens the bottom drawer and there is the lockbox. There is a handgun inside. They had bought it a few years back. He remembers the key is in the bedroom. It's in his sock drawer. He leaves the music room, stops and takes a swig from the vodka bottle on his way through. He goes back upstairs and back into the bedroom and over to the dresser. He starts talking to Andrea on the way. "I need to leave for a while, you just rest." He looks in the drawer and gets the key. "I love you. I'm going to make this right." He goes back down the stairs and into the music room. He goes over to the desk, the drawer with the lock box in it is still open. He reaches in and takes the box out. He puts it on top of the desk, unlocks it and takes out the gun. It is a nine millimeter glock; a cop friend of his in Nevada recommended it when they were having a lot of burglaries in his neighborhood. The clip and ammunition are in the box too. The clip is loaded so he just slides it into place; makes sure the safety is on and sticks it into the waistband of his pants. He turns and leaves the music room and on his way through the living room he grabs a jacket to cover the gun and the bottle of vodka. He goes out to his ford explorer and gets in. He sets his GPS to the address and drives.

When he gets to the house he parks a couple of houses up and on the opposite side of the street. He has only been sitting there a short time when the family comes out; they are all dressed in nice clothes, the mother and daughter in dresses and the father and son in suits, 'a nice looking family' and they climb into the SUV. The same one they used when they went to look at the evil house. When he didn't tell him about the hole in the backyard that would swallow up his child. They look so happy. He gets angrier and angrier. Why has he done this? Because the man is evil too. They pull out of the driveway and head down the street. They go a couple of miles, turning three times and come to a big Baptist church. They pull in and park. George parks across the street and waits.

They are inside a little over an hour. Then everyone starts coming out of the door. David and his family get into the SUV and head back to their house. George follows at a distance and parks back in the same place as before. The family all get out and go in. They stay in the house for about an hour or so. George is drinking out of the bottle of vodka and angrily ranting about the evil man and the evil house. He is saying, you took everything from me and now you just go on your happy way. That's not right! I have to fix it. You took my life away. You took my family. When they come out the woman is carrying a picnic basket, the evil man is carrying an ice chest. The kids have a blanket and a yellow ball. They are dressed casually now. There is a big dog trailing behind them. They all climb back into the SUV. They pull out of the driveway, drive a couple of miles and turn into a parking area at a park. There are swings, slides and a merry-go-round on one side and a picnic area and a pond on the other side. They park on the side with the picnic area. There are picnic tables and grills scattered around the park on this side amongst some shade trees. But there is also a grassy open area where people can play Frisbee or throw a ball around. This is where the pond is. There are also park benches further up by the parking area so people can sit. The evil man and his family get out of the truck and unload the picnic stuff. They make their way down close to the pond. The woman and man lay the blanket on the ground and put all kinds of food on it. They set the ice chest to the side. They sit together on the blanket and the kids and dog run off to play. They are throwing the ball around and the dog is trying to get it away from them. The woman and the evil man sit and talk and watch the ducks glide across the pond. George takes another big swig of vodka and gets out of his explorer and walks over to a water fountain and gets a drink and then he goes over and sits on the bench and watches. That used to be my life, but the evil man took it all away. I must take away his happiness. I must kill his family. To kill his family would be to take his life like he took my life because your life is not that your heart beats, that you breathe, that you can walk around. Your life is what surrounds you. What makes you happy. Like love, beauty and joy. You took my life. Now I must take yours. He becomes angrier and angrier. he gets up, walks down to where the children are, he reaches into his waist band for the gun and pulls it out, clicks the safety off and he roars, "You took everything!" and fires, first he shoots the little girl and then the little boy and then he aims at the woman. They see what is happening and they roll and jump up and run, the woman runs for the children and he shoots her. The man is screaming, "Nooooooooo!" He aims at the man and fires. David feels his breath knocked out of him, he flies back and lands on the ground. He feels a sharp pain in his head and everything goes black. Rufus runs barking and snarling at George and he shoots him too. He just stood there until the police came. When they ask why he had done it he said it was self defense. He was ranting and raving that the evil man had killed him and he had to kill him back.

That was two years ago. Kate, Kelly and Danny all died. He even killed Rufus. I was shot in the shoulder and fell and hit my head on a rock. I was knocked out. He was put into an institution for the criminally insane. They found his wife when they went to his house. Everyone was stunned. His son stayed with his grandmother. It seems I was his monster and he was mine. Everything that I love is gone. So he did kill me sort of. I just watch the couple sitting and talking. The sun is shining, there is a soft breeze. The little boy raises his arms up and spreads his fingers like claws and chases the little girl around growling. They are playing monster. She is running and giggling.

THE END

The Laughing Angel Fish

"Is this my fault?"

Val and Jamie are at the beach again today. They lay on their beach towels working on their tans. They had smoked a joint when they had gotten out of the water and are a little buzzed. They have their beach bag and surf boards on the sand beside them. "Jamie, are you ready to go back in?" He mumbles half asleep, "Yeah" and rolls over on his back and sits up. She does the same and they stand up and grab their boards and run into the water. It is a beautiful day. The waves are just right for surfing. They ride the waves for awhile and then they just lie on their boards and paddle around. They are paddling along when Val sees a cave under a rocky cliff. She says, "Look over there." They start paddling over. It's a couple hundred yards away. When they get close Jamie says, "Cool. Let's explore." Val says, "I don't know man, it looks kinda spooky." "I'll protect you." Jamie says, bending his arm up and showing her his muscle. Val laughs, "My hero."

As they paddle up to the cave the water gets shallower so they get off of their boards and make their way carefully to the cave. There is an outcropping of rock in front and the floor looks like it may be stone. They are carrying their boards by now and they walk up onto the outcropping. They lay their boards down outside the cave and peek inside. It looks to be about eight by ten and is a tunnel with a light at the end. They go in looking all around saying "Wow" and "Cool" They only go about fifty feet or so when the tunnel opens up into a chamber with a fifty foot ceiling. There is an opening that allows sunlight to shine down on a little pool of water with an odd looking statue of a native with eyes the size of saucers. Its lips are pursed and water is flowing out into the pool. The chamber is smaller in diameter. It looks to be about twenty feet or so. The walls are rock. They look at the pool of water and see that it is blue green and clear. It looks to be about five feet across and the sides are sloped like a funnel. When they look closer they see something at the bottom and get down on their knees. It is right in the center of the pool. "What is it?" Val asked. "I don't know, Babe." Jamie says. "We won't be able to reach it without getting in the water." And then Jamie says, "I know, you hold my hand and I'll straddle it and reach down and get it." He asks, "Are you sure? It doesn't look deep." "Yeah, I can do it."

She grabs Jamie's hand and sits on the edge of the pool. She eases over the side and grips the slanted side with her bare foot. She reaches with her other foot for the other side. The water is a little deeper than she thought. Straddled, it was about hip deep. The water is colder than she thought too. "Well, I'm going to have to dunk, it looks like." She says, not looking too thrilled about it. She dunks down and grabs whatever it is, but it won't come loose. It feels like an odd shaped rock. She did feel it slide from side to side. She rose back up for air, and tells Jamie "It's hooked on, but I think I can get it loose." "I'm going to try again." She dunks back down and slides it to one side. It didn't want to move much at first, but then it came loose and it slid out of the grooves that it was in and she came back up gasping. Jamie took what looked like a statue of some sort from her with one hand and pulled her back up out of the water with the other.

They are both sitting on the side of the pool of water looking at the statue. It looks like an angel fish, but it has a big open mouth like its laughing. It's about five inches tall and has little pointed teeth showing. It's black, white and gold and the gold looks to be inlaid. It's pretty, but strange. Val says, "Wow, how cool." Jamie laughs and says, "Yeah, it looks like its high." They both laugh then. They look around some more, but the fountain and pool are about the only things of interest. "Do you think we can keep it?" Val asked. "I won't tell if you won't" Jamie says. So they take the statue and go back to their boards and then back to the beach. Jamie ties it to the draw string on his swimming trunks so he won't lose it. When they make it back to the beach they put it in their beach bag. They gather their stuff together and load everything into their jeep and head to the apartment that they share.

They live in a duplex apartment a couple of miles from the beach. Val is only twenty three and Jamie is twenty five. She works at a coffee shop. Her parents are well off and send her money every month. She would like to open her own coffee shop one day. Jamie works at a surf shop. His parents are divorced and they both send him money too. They joked around about opening a surf and coffee shop. When they go through their apartment door, their St. Bernard Tiny meets them. Jamie says, "Ok boy, I know you need to go out." He tells Val, "I got it" and grabs Tiny's leash and a poop bag so they can go for a walk. They had gotten Tiny as a puppy and trained him from the start so he is very well behaved. While they were out Val took a shower and changed. When she got out of the shower Jamie and Tiny were coming through the door. She was standing beside the table in their little kitchen and she had just pulled out the statue when Tiny went crazy. He started barking and snarling at the statue, but he also wouldn't get very close to it. She looks at Jamie as if saying "What was that?" and she put it back in the bag. She sat on their couch while Jamie took his shower. Tiny had his head in her lap and was looking at the beach bag. He would make a little whimpering sound every once in a while. Jamie came out of the bathroom and stood and looked at Val and Tiny. "I don't know Val, that's strange."

The next day is Saturday. Jamie has to work and Val doesn't. When they wake up the next morning they are lying in bed before it's time to get up. Jamie asks, "So what are you going to do today?" "I think I'll call Susan and see if she wants to have lunch." Susan and Val had been friends for about five years. They met right after Val moved to the coast. Jamie went on to work and Val called Susan. They agree to meet at noon at a little restaurant across the street from her job. Val decides to bring the statue to lunch with her so she can show Susan. She is a little early and orders a margarita and waits. Susan arrives in a flurry of flowers, ruffles and perfume. She is wearing a pink and red flowered, ruffled dress and a big floppy red hat. She works across the street at a flower shop. Val stands up when Susan gets to the table and hugs her. Val says, "Hey, girl, how ya been doin?" Susan replies "I'm doing wonderfulous." Susan is always making up words. They both laugh. "I like that one, I might start using it." They order their lunch and talk and laugh while they eat. Val almost forgets about the statue. But then she says, "Oh yeah, I want to show you something." She reaches into her bag and pulls out the statue. She hands it to Susan and says, "What do you think of this?" When she passes it to her she feels a little electrical shock. Like when you drag your feet on carpet and then touch someone. She doesn't really think about it much. Susan says, "Wow, this is weird, where did you get it?" She holds it up beside her own head and opens her mouth and tries to grin like the fish. Val shakes her head and laughs. "We found it in a cave while we were surfing." "Tiny don't like." All of a sudden Susan says, "It is a little creepy. Here." She hands it back so fast that Val almost drops it. Susan looks at her watch and says, "I've got to go back to work." She bends down and hugs Val. "I'll call you later."

She leaves the restaurant. She has only been out of the door for a minute when Val hears tires screeching. She jumps up and runs out of the restaurant. Out in the middle of the street a group of people have gathered. Outside of the circle of people she can see the red hat. She runs over crying "Is she ok?" "I'm her friend." A man in the circle turns as she comes up and grabs her by the arm. "Ms. I don't think you need to see her. It's bad." He leads her back up onto the sidewalk. All that Val can do is stand on the sidewalk and cry. The police come over and talk to her. The cab driver that had hit her said she just walked out into the road and he didn't have time to stop. The others that witnessed it said it looked like she was sleepwalking or something. The police give her a ride home. She stumbles into the apartment and lands on the couch and just lays there until Jamie gets home. Tiny lies on the floor beside the couch. When Jamie sees her he pulls her up to a sitting position and sits beside her. He puts his arm around her and asks, "What's wrong baby?" "Did you have a bad day?" She starts crying again and tells him what happened. He just holds her and rocks her. After awhile she raises up and says "Ok, I've got to stop this." She calls Susan's mother and talks to her father. They have already heard. The police had called them. Val had told the police how to get a hold of her parents when she had talked to them earlier. She tells them to call if there is anything she can do. Susan's father says that they will let her know when the funeral is going to be.

She puts the statue on the counter in the kitchen area. The next morning when she goes to work she picks it up and sticks it back into her purse. She decides to show it to Macy. She works with her at the coffee shop. She's into zodiac, karma and all kinds of mystical stuff. Maybe she can tell her something about the statue. When she gets there Macy is already behind the counter. She says, "Hi, Val. How ya feelin today? I heard about Susan. It's horrible."Val replies sadly, "I know, I'm shook to the core." Macy says, "I'll cover for you whenever you need, for the funeral or if you just need some time off."Val shakes her head and says, "Thanks" and looks around. There are only a couple of customers so far and they are sitting at the counter. About then the door jingles and Macy starts waiting on the two ladies that come in. Val goes to the back to put on her visor and apron. She comes back out and it isn't long before the customers start coming in steady.

About halfway into her shift they have a chance to take a break. They sit at one of the tables and Val tells Macy about finding the statue. "I'll go get it and show you." She goes to the back and gets it out of her purse. When she gets back she hands it to Macy. Macy gasp as it goes into her hands and hands it back as quickly as she can. "My God Val, that thing just gave me the worst feeling." "I don't know where you got it, but you need to put it back." "I bet it's cursed or something." "Oh my God, I touched it." "I've got to go see if I can find out what it is." She jumps up and runs out of the door without another word. Val sits there stunned. What did she mean? Her friend has always been sort of odd. She can't leave the shop so she calls Jamie and tells him what Macy said and what happened. "Wow, that's crazy." "You know how Macy is, Val, but if you want to take it back we can." Val replies, "Maybe we should, you know with Susan and all, don't' you think? Ok, I'll be off tomorrow and you get off at two so we'll take it back when you get off." Macy doesn't come back and Val tries to call her off and on. Jake comes in at two and takes over. He's the owner and manager. He asks, "Where's Macy?" "She left sick." Val tells him. About then Chris shows up and Val says, "Hi, Chris, I guess I'll go now." She goes to the back and takes off her work stuff and grabs her purse. "You two have a good shift." "See ya tomorrow."

Val decides to go by Macy's apartment and check on her. When she gets there and knocks, no one answers. She is about to knock again when her boyfriend Greg shows up. They live together. Val asks Greg if he has heard from Macy and he says that she called him all hysterical talking about a laughing angel fish. "I didn't know what she was talking about. She was so upset that I rushed home." He has his key out and opens the door. The apartment is quiet. Val follows Greg in. They both look around. They look in the other rooms. Everything seems normal. Where could she be? Greg notices the window open in the living room. He says, "That was closed when we left. I wonder where she is." They notice a book open on the coffee table. Val looks at the cover. It is a book about ancient curses and idles. "I thought she was calling from home. She was talking about trying to find an antidote for a curse. She was rambling on so I couldn't understand her." He walks over to the window then and was about to close it when he looks out and says, "Oh no, she's down there lying on the ground. She must have fallen." There is an alley on this side of the apartment and they both run down to where she is lying motionless on the ground. Her head is at an odd angle and her eyes are open and blank. She is dead.

They called 911 and before they know it there are EMT's and police everyone. They couldn't determine how she went out the window. There was no evidence that she was pushed, but they couldn't figure out how a healthy twenty two year old could just fall out of a window either. All of the way back to her apartment she cries and wonders, "Is this my fault?" She has never been superstitious. She doesn't know what to think. She just knows that they have to get rid of the statue. When Jamie arrives home she tells him everything. He can't believe it. He isn't the superstitious type either, but he is also thinking it wouldn't hurt to take it back. Val calls the coffee shop and tells

Jake what happened. She asks if she can take the next day off to recuperate. He says he would cover for her. When she moves the statue from her purse to the beach bag she uses a paper towel. She can't bring herself to touch it. They decide to take it back in the morning.

The next morning they get up and have coffee and breakfast. They dress for the beach and leave. It is around nine o'clock when they arrive at the beach. They brought a fanny pack to carry the statue in when they surf out to the cave. Val still isn't touching it even though she had in the beginning. She uses a paper towel to move it from the beach bag to the fanny pack and stuffs the paper towels in another small pocket in the fanny pack. Jamie wears it on their trip out to the cave. When they get close they notice that it doesn't look the same. They can't even see the entrance to the cave this time. Val gets a sinking feeling when Jamie says, "Where did it go?" Val says, "I don't know." They get a little closer and they can see that the entrance to the cave has been covered. It looks like the ceiling of the cave has fallen in. It just looks like a big pile of rocks. The outcropping is covered with huge boulders and they can't even climb out of the water. There is nowhere to stand. "What are we going to do?" Val asks.

They go back to the beach and sit on the towels that they had put in the beach bag. Jamie pulls out a joint and they smoke it while they discuss what to do. "Well, we can leave it at the pile of rocks," Val says. "Yeah, I guess you're right. We can just throw it up on top."Jamie says. That's what they decide to do. They go back out and get up close to it and Jamie throws it as far up on the pile of rocks as he can. It lands, wobbles and then settles. Jamie and Val say together, "All right!" and high five. They turn around and head back to the beach. When they get there they load their stuff into the jeep and go back to their apartment.

The rest of their day is pretty mellow. They stay high. Before they go to bed Val is emptying out the beach bag. When she pulls the towels out, the statue tumbles out and lands on the floor. She looks down and sees that goofy grin and it is terrifying. Tiny runs off to the bedroom like he is scared to death. Val can't believe it. Jamie is sitting on the couch looking stunned. Val stumbles over to the couch, flops down and says, "Am I going crazy, Jamie. How did that happen?" She feels dizzy and like she needs to throw up. Jamie says, "I don't know?" "This is crazy." Val says, "What do we do?" "Do we take it back out? Do we burn it? Do we take it to a priest? Jamie picks it up and puts it in the fanny pack. He uses a paper towel this time. He put the fanny pack in the closet in their bedroom. They sit there talking for an hour or so. They decide that they won't show it to anyone else until they know more about it and finally they go to bed.

They go to the funerals. They go to work and to the beach. They do their usual things. One day when Val is walking home from the coffee shop she notices that a book store is opening in an old house not far from her job. She sees the sign going up and it reads "The Magic Carpet." The signs in the windows read "We have some of most rare books around." "Collectors come look." She finds herself going in without even thinking about it. There is an older man behind the counter. He has long hair tied back and a mustache and beard. He is pulling books out of a box and reading the binds. She scans some of the titles as she walks up and sees "Rare Exotic Archeological Finds" "Rights of Passage" "Indian Rituals" She thinks, "Perfect." She starts talking to the man and discovers the shop would be opening in a week. She asks him about the books on the counter and says that she and her boyfriend had found something really unusual and they need to find out about it. This gets the guy going. He says his name is Mike and asks

"So, what do you have?" She finds herself telling him all about the statue and everything that has happened. When she is done, he is quiet. He says, "I think I have read something about a fish statue like the one you describe." "It's been awhile, let me look around and see if I can find it." "As you see I haven't got everything set up or unpacked. This sounds serious though so I'm going to try to find the material as quickly as I can." "Can you come back by tomorrow?" Val's heart is beating fast; this has been on their minds since Macy. Finally, maybe they'll get some answers. She says, "Of course, how about the same time tomorrow?"

She leaves the store and walks the rest of the way home thinking about finding answers. She tells Jamie when he arrives home and he is relieved like she is to finally be doing something. They hadn't even wanted to look at it since the night they put it in the fanny pack. The next day Val takes the fanny pack to work with her so she can show Mike. They had hired someone else for Macy's position. Everyone is still mourning her though. The new girl's name is Jodie and she seems nice although sometimes she is a little invasive. She asks a lot of questions, sometimes too many and Val figures she is just trying too hard to be friendly. She sees Val when she comes in and asks her "What's with the fanny pack?" "Oh it's nothing, it's just something I found and am trying to get rid of."

Later on when they are working, curiosity gets the best of her and she sneaks to the back to take a look. Val has put her things in a little cubby hole on the desk in Jakes office. They all usually go in and out of this area because some of the supplies are stored there. They have always trusted each other so she didn't think anyone would mess with the fanny pack. Jodie stands at the desk and opens the fanny pack. She sees the statue inside and pulls it out. She is holding it when she feels the zap to her hand. It was like a tiny little shock and it scared her. She puts it back immediately and goes back to the front and Val notices that she doesn't look right. She's pale and seems nervous. Jodie tells Jake and Val that she doesn't feel well and needs to leave. Jake looks at Val and shrugs. She has just had time to get out of the door when they hear a huge crash. They run to the door, open it and stop. There on the ground is Jodie with a big shard of glass sticking out of her back and others scattered all around her. There is no chance that she has survived. They go back in and call 911.

Val goes to the back feeling sick and looks at the fanny pack. The zipper is open. Val starts crying and can't stop. She finally calms down enough to talk to the police and they tell her that a plate glass window three stories up had fallen out. They didn't understand how it could have happened but they are going to investigate. As soon as the police leave Val tells Jake that she can't stay and he says that he understands. She carefully zips the fanny pack, grabs her things and runs out the door. She calls Jamie and tells him what has happened, crying all the way through it. He tells her that he will meet her at the apartment at three. He says he can't leave because the other guy is out. She goes straight to the bookstore hoping that Mike is there. She is a little early, it is only eleven o'clock.

He is there behind the counter on the floor reading a book when Val comes in. The bell over the door jingles and Mike rises up from behind the counter. Val looks terrible; her eyes are puffy and red. Mike asks, "How's it going or should I ask?" She shakes her head. "I have to get rid of it." "There's been another accident." Mike tells her to come around the counter. There is quite a bit of space back there. She spots a chair and sits down. She tells him about what had happened. He sits back down on the floor and picks up the book that he had been reading. "I found this book. It's called "Old Indian Myths, Are

They Real?" There is a story in here about the Laughing Angel Fish. It tells a story about an Indian chief who lost his woman during child birth. He so loved this woman that it just about killed him when she died. The baby survived. It was a little boy. The tribe lived in a village close to the coast and were fishermen. When the boy was about twelve years old the chief had a dispute with another tribe. The chief of the other tribe had heard about him losing his woman and how it almost destroyed him and how now the son that they had created together was the most important thing to him. He threatened to kill the boy if he didn't give in. The story goes that the chief went to the Big Water and prayed to the Great Fish God. The fish statue washed up on the shore and the Great Fish God told him to give it to his son. The statue would protect him. He told him that after the statue went into the hands of his son that no one other than himself could touch it without dying. The statue looks happy so people will not be afraid of it. The father took the statue back to the camp and gave it to his son. He told him that he must not let anyone else see it. He told him that there were men wanting to kill him and if they came up on him to offer the statue in trade for his life. The statue was so beautiful that they would want it.

The chief of the other tribe sent warriors to kill the boy. They came up on him while he was out of the others sight. He had gone off to pick some berries on the edge of their village. He had the statue in a leather pouch tied around his waist and didn't have time to get it out. They killed him and left him there. When they found him his father went crazy. He raged and cried out that he was going to get his revenge. They had a big ceremony and burnt the boy's body on a pyre and prayed to the tribes fishermen gods. They took his ashes to a cave on the shore of the big water and built a monument with a statue that sees all and a fountain so the boy will never thirst. He left the statue at the bottom of the fountain. That evening when the men sat around their fire, they made plans to attack the village of the tribe that killed his son. The next morning they went to the other village right before sunrise and attacked. The other tribe was caught completely off guard and they wiped out most of the warriors.

Mike says "That's about it." And Val asks, "How come it hasn't been discovered before?" Mike replies, "It may be that it was covered with rocks and when the cliff washed away it opened back up or even mild quakes." Val says "I wonder what we can do now." "I'll have to do some research." Mike replies. You just go home and get your boyfriend and I'll keep working on it. Val says, "He'll be home at about three and we can come back over then and help?" Mike tells her, "Sounds good to me."

Val goes straight home and waits on Jamie. When he arrives home she tells him what she had found out about the statue. They head back over to the book store. When they arrive Mike is still sitting behind the counter, but this time he is sitting on the chair. Val introduces Jamie to Mike and the brain storming begins. Mike tells them that what he had found before was all that he had seen so far about the Laughing Angel Fish, but from other Indian myths and beliefs he thinks that they need to take it back. Val says, "We've tried that." Mike says, "I think that you need to bury it this time." "The chief's intentions were that the statue would protect his son in the afterlife." "I think it is important that the statue be under the ground with the son." Jamie says, "I think you're right." Val is shaking her head, "Ok." Jamie looks at Val and says, "Let's do this." They walk back to their apartment and gather the tools that they will need to bury it.

This time they tie their kayak to the top of the jeep. When they arrive at the beach they unload everything and set out for the collapsed cave. When they get to the cave, they tie the boat to a little tree growing out of the rocks and they climb up to the top of the pile. They estimate about where the fountain was and start removing rocks and dirt. There are a lot of rocks and chunks of earth to move so it takes them about an hour to get two feet. They keep digging and in another hour they are about four feet down. They open up the fanny pack and carefully dump the statue into the hole. It takes another hour to cover it up. They put all of the dirt and rocks that they had taken out back in. When they are done the sun had already started going down. They make their way back down the pile and load their tools in the kayak and go back to the beach. They are quiet all of the way. Both of them thinking "Please stay there."

They make it to the beach, load the jeep, and then hold each other in a long hug. They went home exhausted, showered and fell into their bed. They woke the next morning still tired and anxious. They both have to work but before they leave they look in the beach bag and the statue isn't in it. The whole day they are afraid that it will come back. On the way home Val stops by the book store and tells Mike about their evening. He pats her on the back and reassures her that it is going to be ok. As she leaves he tells her "It's over, go home and relax."

That evening at their apartment they did start to relax. They were sitting on their couch smoking a joint and watching TV when they felt the earth shake. It was an earthquake. When it was over they just looked at each other. It was only a 3.0 quake so there wasn't much damage. Just a couple of broken windows and some of the cliffs had fallen into the ocean.

THE END

HORSE SENSE

The eyes see clearer when the heart is open.

Clyde sits by his fire dreaming. I have a good feeling about this, he thinks. He had left their old shack farm house outside of Oklahoma City about two and a half months before looking for work. He had left his mother, brothers and sisters out there. Joseph is fifteen, Luke twelve, Rose five and Emily is only two. His father had passed last winter. He figured he would find work and send money home or make enough to set them up somewhere else. Clyde had just turned eighteen last month. He had to leave so he could find a way to get his family away from their used up, worn out farm now that Pa is gone. His Ma had cried when he left, it broke her heart for him to go, after Pa. In her eyes though he could see that she knew, it was what he had to do. There isn't any work to be had there, at least not for a wet behind the ears kid like him. Joseph can take care of things at home with their three puny chickens and old Betsy, their milk cow. He left Pa's rifle so he could hunt too.

He had talked to a blacksmith in Tulsa about work and he had told him about the gold in the Black Hills of South Dakota. He let him stay at the blacksmith shack and work for a couple of weeks, just enough to buy some supplies, beans, rope, a pickax and a shovel. He would go stake a claim. Make it where his family wouldn't have to struggle anymore. He decided when he got to Kansas City he would follow the Missouri River up into South Dakota so he could camp along the river and have plenty of water and fish to eat. He can hunt rabbits, squirrels or whatever else he can see too. He'd brought his old hunting rifle. He had gotten it when he was ten and his Pa had started letting him hunt with him. He loved those times. Clyde wanted to cry just thinking about his Pa. Now it's just him and his old mule Jack. He feels lonely thinking about his family. He didn't leave Jack; nothing would grow on their farm anyway. They already had to sell their plow just to survive the winter. Pa was sick a long time. It just seemed to come on. He got more tired every day and then he went to bed and never got up. He was bed ridden for about three months or so. He was in such pain and misery that when he died, it was a sad relief. The Doctor came out to the farm once from Oklahoma City, and said he had cancer.

Clyde figures he's probably about half ways between Tulsa and Kansas City. He's camped beside a boulder, just sitting, gazing into the fire and thinking, when he hears a noise. He automatically grabs his rifle and looks around, it sounds like hooves on ground, and the sound is coming from behind him on the other side of the boulder. He slowly eases up and looks into the darkness on the other side. He stays low so he won't be seen. His heart is beating hard in his chest and he is holding his breath. He squints his eyes trying to see and there is a movement a little ways in. He stays really still and slowly raises his rifle up and points it at a dim shadow in the darkness. He stays quiet and watches. The shadow moves slightly, he says, "Stop right there or I'll shoot." Old Jack is shuffling around. He feels the tension. The shadow moves again, coming closer. It looks like a horse, a palomino. He raises his eyes. It doesn't look like there is a rider. The shadow moves again. He can see it is a horse. No rider. It snorts. Jake just looks, surprised. A lone horse, just wondering up. The horse starts moving again. It is coming around the boulder. Clyde slowly turns as the horse comes around. When the horse is all the way around it stops and just stands there.

From what he can see with the light of the campfire and the moon it is a healthy looking palomino horse. A stallion. He can see developed muscles under a shiny coat. Clyde wonders where the rider is. There is no bridle or saddle. He is half standing and trying to look everywhere at once and listening. Nothing. He eases to his right and moves slowly around the boulder, he crouches down and looks hard into the dark. He yells, "Come out now or I'll shoot your horse." He wouldn't really shoot the horse, but he didn't have anything else to threaten. He waits like that for about a half hour. Nothing. I can't wait all night like this he thinks. He eases back around the boulder very quietly, watching. When he had made it back around he looks at the horse. "Where did you come from?" He asks. He slowly edges his way closer. He reaches the front side of the horse. He puts his hand out and gently pets the side of the horse's neck. The horse just stands there. He pets some more. He seems tame and he eases around to the front of the horse. The horse's eyes are just amazing in their intelligence. He has the look of an old soul. He asks again "Where did you come from?" He pets the horse's nose and talks soothingly to him. He seems completely tame. He walks over to Jack and pulls a rope off that he has tied to his saddle. He unwinds several feet and ties a slip knot in it. He puts the rope around the horse's neck and closes the loop some. He just stands there, it seemed like he lowered his head into the loop when he was putting it on him. He leads him over to where he has Jack tied and ties him up there too. He goes back to where he was sitting beside the fire earlier and sits back down. He just looks at the horse. "Where did you come from?" He didn't see any kind of markings on the horse, but he's tame. He figures it's getting late. He says out loud "Early day tomorrow, better get some sleep". He lays out his blanket and wraps it around himself. He lays there awhile and listens to the night.

Everything is quiet. He has his rifle in his hand under his blanket. He sleeps.

When he wakes up it is light already and he had slept soundly. He sees the horse standing next to Jack. At first he had thought he might have dreamed it. He gets up, rolls up his blanket and ties it to Jacks saddle. He gathers his stuff and ties it to the saddle too. He walks down about twenty yards to a stream where he washes his face. As he walks back up to his camp he wonders "How am I going to travel with this horse and a mule? I'm not even sure I can ride the horse yet." He decides to try it anyway. He unloads Jacks saddle, removes the saddle, blanket and the bridle and slowly he moves toward the palomino with it. First he puts the blanket on and the horse just stands there calmly. Then he raises the saddle up and places it on the horses back and adjusts the bridle. The horse acts as if he is familiar with saddles. He has to adjust the straps to make them fit better and the horse stays calm. He decides to use his rope and his sleeping blanket to tie the rest of his supplies and mining gear that he had gathered in Tulsa onto Jack. He knows Jack is used to it. He has Jack loaded and he ties him to the saddle. He very carefully climbs up on the saddle and says "Git up" clicks and nudges the horse's sides with his boots and they start moving.

They start off at a walking pace, he nudges him with his feet again and they speed up to a slow gallop. He doesn't know if Jack can keep up if they go too fast so they find a nice fast walking pace and move along through the countryside. As they go Clyde talks to Jack and the horse about how they are going to get to the Black Hills and find a claim that is so full of gold that him and his family will be able to settle on a nice rich piece of land and never want for anything ever again. He told them how he would buy his Ma a beautiful new dress. He doesn't remember her ever having one. "And one for Rose and

Emily too and dolls and a new pair of overalls for Joseph and Luke and candy." "I wonder what I can call you horse, you need a name." "Let me think.....I know, I'll call you Ben after my Pa." So they travel along, Clyde talking to Jack and Ben the whole way.

That evening they make camp in a good spot with a creek not far away and cover close by in case they need it. He takes his rifle and goes out into the woods to see if he can spot a rabbit or a squirrel. He shoots a rabbit, skins and guts it away from the camp and takes it to the creek to wash it. He finds two forked sticks and another longer straight one. He uses his whittling knife to sharpen the ends of the straight stick and pierces the rabbit with it. He then cooks the rabbit over an open fire. He enjoys sitting by his fire as the sun goes down with his rabbit cooking. Just gazing up at the sky and thinking about his family. He eats his rabbit while Ben and Jack graze close by. After awhile he lies down under the stars and goes to sleep.

The next day is when things got strange. Clyde, Jack and Ben are traveling along when Ben starts to get agitated. He stops at a creek so they can drink, climbs down and looks at Ben. If a horse could look like crying Ben did. He looks so sad. Clyde thinks maybe he's getting tired of being tied to Jack and needs to take a little run. He unties him from Jack and ties Jack to a tree in a shade by the creek. He had seen a clearing back the way they had come so he slings his rifle over his shoulder, climbs onto Ben's back and rides back the way they had come. They are trotting along when all of a sudden Ben speeds up and starts running faster than Clyde has ever moved on a horse before. He is running in the direction of the clearing, when they get to the field from earlier, Ben starts across; they veer off to the right and out of the clearing onto a path through some trees. Up ahead he can see a little old cabin. On the porch there is a little girl about Roses age, she is backed up against the house too far from the door to run in and a wolf is getting ready to attack. His shackles are up and he is snarling with evil looking teeth showing. The little girl is crying. As he comes up Ben goes to the side a little, Clyde raises his rifle and shoots. The wolf is shot in the head and dies immediately.

 He hadn't even noticed the woman that had been standing in the door of the cabin. She runs to the little girl and pulls her into her arms, both of them crying hysterically. Clyde climbs down from Ben and stands there watching. After they calm down some, the woman turns as if just noticing Clyde standing there. She has tears running down her face and is holding the little girl on her hip. She says, "You saved my baby." He tells her, "I'm glad I was able to help." About that time a man and a little boy come out of the woods. They are carrying rifles and a couple of dead rabbits. The man drops the rabbits and raises his gun and points it at Clyde. He sees the woman and the little girl crying and says, "What's going on here?" The man looks at him and then at the woman. The boy runs over to the woman and little girl as if to protect them. She says, "He saved Mary's life." The man notices the dead wolf lying on their porch and lowers the rifle. He walks toward Clyde with his hand out saying "I don't know how to thank you." They introduce themselves, they are Tom and Eve, and the little boy is John and ten years old. He had just started hunting with his father. They invite him to stay and eat dinner with them; he goes back and gets Jack. Eve cooks rabbit stew and hard rolls. It is the best meal he has eaten since leaving home. After eating they all sit around the table and talk. They tell him about their life in the cabin in the woods. Clyde tells them about the family he had left behind and his plans to stake a claim and find gold. There was a little barn out back. They let him put Jack and

Ben out there and they let him sleep in front of their fire. The next morning they had to leave.

Before he left, Eve wraps up some hard rolls, and they tell him if he ever comes through again to stop by. It's time to head out again. He is missing home more than ever. As he is riding across the clearing he starts thinking about the day before. How did Ben know to take him to that cabin? It was strange. He put it out of his mind until the next time.

They had been traveling for a couple of weeks from the cabin when Ben starts acting restless again. They stop again and Clyde ties Jack to a tree in a good hidden place by water. He remembers the last time. He looks into Bens eyes and there is that sad look again. So he grabs his rifle and slings it over his shoulder and jumps on Ben. They shoot off like a bullet. By this time they are almost to Kansas City and that is the direction they are going. They head right into the city. It is loud and busy. He hadn't been around many people in a while, it felt strange. Ben swings to the left and into an alley and there is the back of a man and he has a woman on the ground. He has her skirt raised and she is fighting. He has a knife to her throat. He is trying to get her under clothes down with his other hand. They stop right at their feet. He is sitting on Ben and he points his rifle at the man and says "get up now" in his angriest voice. The man jumps up, this all happens really fast. The woman is pulling her dress down and scooting backwards crying. She's an older lady. He tells him to drop the knife and to leave before he shoots him. The man is cussing and saying he'll get him. He's slurring and staggering. His pants are open and he doesn't even realize it. He staggers out of the alley. As he passes Clyde can smell the corn liquor. He jumps down and the woman is still crying like she's scared to death. He walks over slowly, talking, telling her she's going to be ok. He helps her up and asks her to tell him where she needs to go. She says to her daughter's house around the corner. They walk out of the alley and down the street. Ben follows right behind them. They turn once and there stands a white house with flower beds, a white picket fence and a porch. There is a woman and a man sitting on the porch. They both jump up when they see them. The woman is screaming. "What are you doing to my Mama?" The man is yelling "turn her loose". They are both running towards him. He is getting scared. All of a sudden the woman realizes what they are thinking and puts her hand up yelling "stop he's helping me". When they reach them the woman's daughter takes her mother up onto the porch. The daughter is holding what looks like a straw hat in her hand. She sits her down and gets her to tell her what happened. The man stays down on the street and Clyde tells him what he came up on in the alley. Clyde takes Ben's reins and leads him up to the step railing and ties him there. They walk up onto the porch and he tells the women that he needs to go get the sheriff. Jake goes with him. They walk down the street about a quarter of a mile to the sheriff's office. On the way they talk and the man tells him that his name is William Thomas and his wife is Melissa. He says that the older woman is his wife's mother. Her name is Mrs. Joanne Bagley. They had just come outside and seen that she was gone. Earlier she had been working in the flower beds.

As it turned out the man was a local troublemaker who had staggered from the saloon about a half hour earlier. He saw Mrs. Bagley out in the yard and had dragged her down the street and into the alley. The sheriff knew who it was as soon as Clyde described him. When he was picked up he said he didn't remember anything. He was passed out in a ditch with his pants still open and some of Mrs. Bagley's hair still in his hand. When Clyde was asked how he found them he said he heard the struggle and went down the alley. He didn't try to explain how he ended up in town.

Clyde told them he needed to go get his mule. He was beginning to worry because they had been gone for awhile. They thanked him profusely and told him if he ever came through again to stop in. He said he would and he rode off on Ben. It was getting late and Jack had been left for awhile. Clyde didn't know what to do about it though. When Ben needed him to go they went and it was always urgent. When they got back to Jack, he was still tied to the tree. Clyde was relieved that Jack was alright. He decided to camp there for the night so he tied Ben beside Jack. He looked at the horse and said "I don't know how you do it you crazy old horse" laughed and shook his head. I've got to go get some grub. Clyde would let Ben and Jack graze along the way whenever he came across a nice grassy spot. They had stopped earlier before their wild ride into town. He would let them eat again while he cooked. He went into the woods and shot a squirrel for his supper. While he roasted it over the fire he let Ben and Jack graze. There was a nice little patch of grass right next to where they are camped. He ate his supper and slept under the clear night sky.

The next morning they headed back toward Kansas City. When they get there, they started following the Missouri River. By that evening they had made it into Nebraska. They camp on the river. The water looks dangerous. That evening Clyde finds a pole and fishes for his supper. He catches a nice catfish and cooks it over his fire. They have a quiet evening and go to sleep early so they can get an early start. The next day they make their way up the river. They had been going all day. By looking at the sun it looks like it might be about six o'clock or so. They find a good place beside the river to camp. Clyde is making a fire and he has tied Ben and Jack to a tree. Clyde hears Ben snort and looks up and sees that usual look and agitation that means they need to go do something. He grabs his rifle, this time Ben's saddle is already off so he just jumps on him bare back. He grabs a hold of his mane and they take off. They go up the river about a half mile and Ben stops. They are facing the river and he hears yelling coming from that direction. He looks out and sees someone in the river. This person is bobbing and yelling and being washed down river. Clyde is thinking fast. His rope is back at camp and as luck would have it that is the direction this person is going. He heads back down river toward his camp. They are moving as fast as they can. As they go he looks over and sees this person being washed along. It is like they were racing. He reaches camp and he jumps off and grabs his rope. He looks around. He is looking for something that will float. Just then he sees a big piece of drift wood. It is about ten or fifteen feet from the edge of the river and about three feet long and six inches wide. He runs over and picks it up and it is dry and light. It might work. He ties one end of the rope to the piece of wood and winds the rest loosely in his other hand. He hopes it will be long enough. He runs back up river looking and listening. Just a little ways up he sees the head bobbing and yells "Over here, try to get as close to bank as you can." It looks like a young boy. His arms are waving and it looks like he is trying to make his way over. The current is pulling him down river, Clyde is going to lose him if he doesn't do something fast. He let some slack in the rope and swings it around like a sling and let it fly. He tries throwing it down river, to the other side so the wood will float across his path. All of the time he is yelling what he is doing to the boy out in the river. The second try works. He grabs hold of the driftwood and then the rope and Clyde pulls him in.

The boy in the river is fourteen and lives about a mile away. Clyde gets him back to his camp and they sit beside the fire so he can dry. He had run away from home. His situation is similar to Clyde's. His name is Jim and he had left home to find a way for his family to survive. With him though, his father is alive. They are just having a hard time like everyone else at this time and from talking to him it sounds like he has a lot of sisters and brothers. Jim left home to find gold. His Pa had told him he is too young to leave home yet. Clyde talks to him and tells him how his Pa had passed and about how much he misses him and his family. He tells him he will feel so alone and miss them so badly that it will be like a physical pain. Like a stab in the heart. The boy decides he will go back home, at least until he gets older. He stays by the river that night. The next morning Clyde goes with him to his farm so he can meet his family.

They set out the next morning at day break. Jim rides behind Clyde on Ben. It takes about an hour to reach Jims farm. As they ride up Clyde sees a dilapidated old wooden house. There is smoke coming out of the chimney. As they get up close to the house a woman, a man and a whole bunch of kids run out. The woman is crying and yelling "Where have you been? We have been worried sick." When they stop Jim jumps down and his mother grabs him and hugs him. His father is standing beside her with a stern look on his face. The kids, there must be ten of them at least are running everywhere. After things calm down some Jim introduces Clyde to his family. The kids are all different ages from a baby that one of his sisters is holding to Jim. They are all petting Jack and it looks like he is enjoying it as much as they are. They are very poor. They have a milk cow and a garden. Clyde notices an old plow off to the side of the yard with weeds growing up around it. After talking to Jim he discovers that their mule had died a few months back and they don't have the money to get another one. After a lot of thought and a lot of heartache Clyde decides to leave

Jack with Jim's family. They are so thankful for the help and tell Clyde that they will take good care of him. He tells them that when he gets some money he will buy a mule and bring it back and pick Jack up then. He loads all of his stuff onto Ben. Before he leaves he has a talk with Jack and explains that Jim's family needs his help and that he will be back to get him. He cries as he rides off on Ben. Jack is part of the home he had left behind.

Clyde is really sad about leaving Jack. He cries for awhile as he goes. They travel up the river until the sun starts going down and then they make camp. Clyde lets Ben graze as he fishes for his supper. He catches a medium size catfish. He isn't feeling very hungry. He is still sad about Jack. He only eats a little of his fish and he throws the rest into the river. He lays down to sleep that night feeling lonelier than he has felt since he left home. He awakens the next morning still sad, but he knows that he isn't that far from South Dakota. They solemnly head up river. He knows from talking to the blacksmith in Tulsa that the Missouri River will take him right into South Dakota. He will need to head Northwest to Sioux Falls and then he will go west to Rapid City. They make it into South Dakota about three days later at sun down. They made better time without Jack. He camps beside the river knowing that the next morning he will be heading away from the river and towards Sioux City. He shoots a squirrel for his supper. He's getting tired of fish. He sits by his fire talking to Ben while he eats. He talks to him about missing Jack and his family. He tells Ben that it is just the two of them now, but they will strike it rich and go back and get Jack and his family and they will find a nice place to live. Everything will be wonderful then. He has trouble falling asleep that night. His mind just keeps going over and over all that has happened so far and he is getting excited about going into town. He has heard that it is pretty rough there. The blacksmith told him he best just stay quiet and not draw too much attention to himself.

The next morning they head to the city of Sioux Falls. They arrive there a little after noon. It is loud and busy. There is saloon music playing and yelling, laughing and fighting. There are people hawking their wares. He can hear "Picks, Pans, Boots, anything you'll need to get that gold right here!" There are fancy women everywhere. He hasn't ever seen one in real life, but he had heard about them from the boys he had grown up with. He stops Ben in the middle of the road and is just looking around. He hasn't ever seen anything like it in his life. So busy. About then someone yells "Get out of my way or I'll run you over, you stupid kid." Clyde is startled. He gets moving then, out of the middle of the road. About then a woman says in a solicitous purr, "Hey kid how bout you buy your first piece, I'll be gentle." and she laughs. There are a couple of other women standing with her and they laugh too. He decides he needs go somewhere out of the open. He maneuvers Ben through the crowd not sure where he's going. He knows that he needs to get to the outskirts of the city where he can camp. He heads back the way he had come. When he reaches the edge of town he feels relieved. He decides to go ahead west until the sun starts to go down and then find a place to camp and a place to think. A while later in the evening he sits beside his fire and listens to the coyotes howl in the distance and talks to Ben."Well, we're headed to our final destination now." I figure if we make good time we should get there before winter comes. He lay under the stars that night thinking about the city and how strange everything was there. He thinks about the painted ladies and about meeting someone one day and falling in love. He finally falls asleep with these thoughts going through his head.

The next morning they head west toward Rapid City. They have been going across prairie land for a long time, ever since they left the river. They are going along carefully because of the rough terrain and all of the prairie dog holes. Clyde has lost track of how many days they have been traveling, it feels like seven or eight, when Ben starts acting strange again. They are going along and Ben stops and snorts and off they go. Clyde is worried about Ben going so fast. They swing to the right through some low bushes and Ben stops. There is a young Indian boy lying on the ground unconscious and a rock beside his head that has blood on it. The boy's horse has fallen in a hole and is laid over on its side. It looks like its leg is broken. Clyde walks over to the boy and squats down. He puts his hand on his chest. He feels his chest rise and fall. He's breathing; he can feel a heartbeat too. He looks at his head and sees that there is a gash there. His horses' leg is bent at the wrong angle. He knows what he has to do, and it breaks his heart. He doesn't waste any time, he walks over to the horse, raises his rifle and shoots him in the head. He cries while he does this. He tries to get himself together before he turns back around in case the boy woke up. He hadn't. He sees a creek down the hill some. He looks in his saddle bag for his one extra shirt and tears a small piece off the bottom. He takes it down to the creek and wets it. The water is cold. He has noticed that it is getting colder. He takes the wet clothe back up and sits on the ground and washes the boys face. The boy starts coming to. He sees Clyde and tries to jump up, but his head is hurting too bad. He lies there looking like he is scared to death. Clyde starts talking to him, not knowing if he understands or not. He tells him "I am a friend, it's okay." "My name is Clyde." "Do you understand me?" The boy looks like he is calming down some. He says "I understand." My tribe calls me Star Watcher." "I have learned white man's language." "Where is my horse?" He starts looking around slowly then.

He sees his horse on the ground dead and his eyes tear up and a tear rolls down his cheek. The boy looks to be about ten years old or so. Clyde tells him "I'm so sorry." "His leg was broke real bad. I had to." He was crying again too. Dang it, he wiped his eyes on his shirt sleeve thinking, I'm supposed to be grown up. He asks if he feels like he can sit up. He says yes and slowly sits. They turn their backs to the dead horse; neither of them wants to see it. Clyde asks him where he lives. Star Watcher tells him that he doesn't live far away. Just over that next hill. Clyde tells him he will let him ride with him on Ben since his head is still pretty sore and he takes him to his reservation.

When they get there everyone turns and slowly starts walking in their direction. Before he knows it they are surrounded by Indians. Star Watcher speaks to his people in their language. One of the Indians looks like he may be the chief. He steps forward and speaks in English. Thank you for bringing Star Watcher home. He turns to a couple of warriors and speaks to them. They come up beside them and reach for Star Watcher. As he is getting off of Ben he says, "They are taking me to the medicine man. Thank you, friend. You know we are friends forever now." The chief says "Stay and sit for a while." Clyde climbs down. They all gather around their fire and sit down. Clyde joins them. The chief ask about the horse and he tells them about how he had to shoot it. He feels like crying again just telling the story. The chief speaks to a couple of young warriors and they leave. He tells Clyde that they will take care of the horse. "You must stay and eat with us this evening. The women are already preparing food for you to say thank you." Another Indian brave comes up and sits next to the chief and talks to him. He is holding what looks like a large wolf hide. The chief interprets for him. "This is Bird Man, he is Star Watchers father." "He wants me to tell you that you have given him his son and he is forever grateful." He wants you to have this wolf fur to keep you warm in your travels. After awhile the women start bringing food out. One Indian woman comes up with a piece of bark loaded with roasted deer, wild onions, roots and greens of some kind. The chief tells Clyde that she is Star Watcher's mother. Her name is Butterfly Woman. During the evening she takes him into a teepee and lets him see Star Watcher. He has his head bandaged now, but looks good. He tells Clyde that his mother is making him rest. They ask him to stay that night at the reservation. They play celebration drums and dance around the fire. He is told he will sleep in Star Watcher's family's teepee. He ties Ben with their horses and before he goes he looks into Ben's eyes and says "You are something. I just don't know." He reaches in and hugs the horse. He goes into their teepee and Star Watcher is lying awake. He is sad about his horse. He shows him where his mother had put an animal skin on the ground for him to sleep. He talks to Star Watcher for a while. Star Watcher tells him about life on the reservation and about their beliefs that when people die they come back as different creatures. It makes Clyde wonder if maybe Ben had been human in a past life. After awhile Star Watcher is quiet. He hears Bird Man and Butterfly Woman come in and bed down for the night. He finally falls asleep in the early morning hours.

He awakens later than usual feeling tired. He tells all of his new friends good bye. Butterfly woman wraps a piece of deer meat in a large leaf and pats him on the arm. He just nods at everyone and they nod back. Before he climbs onto Ben he rolls up his new fur and ties it to his saddle and then he looks into Bens eyes. He sees that intelligence again and wonders "Where did you come from?" He climbs on and they start heading west again. It is feeling colder. It must be getting close to winter again. He is wearing his extra shirt and long underwear. He has to put on his heavy coat. That night he spreads out the horse blanket and covers Ben with it. He wraps himself up in his blanket and he wraps the wolf fur around himself too. He has Ben move in as close to the fire as he can. He is worn out from his lack of sleep at the reservation the night before. He sleeps soundly.

They had been traveling like this for about two weeks when Ben did it again. The weather had gotten even colder and it had snowed the night before. They are moving along. Clyde has been getting really lonely. He hasn't seen anyone since he had left Star Watcher's reservation. He is talking to Ben, 'he does that a lot' when all of a sudden Ben stops as if he is startled. He snorts and starts galloping to the north. They go about a mile and come up on what looks like a wagon trail. They go up the trail a little ways and there 'where the trail slopes down on the sides' he sees an overturned wagon. There is a young woman wearing a dark brown wool cape with a hood sitting on the ground on the other side of the wagon crying. When she sees Clyde she starts yelling that her father is trapped under the wagon. Clyde jumps down from Ben and eases down the steep embankment. He goes around the wagon and there he sees an older man and his legs are underneath the wagon. The wagon has landed on its side trapping the man's legs underneath. He is conscious so he kneels and says. "Sir, I'm going to get this wagon off of you." He shakes his head. He looks like he is in pain. Clyde looks back and forth between the girl and the man as he talks. I'm going to tie a rope to this side of the wagon and the other end to my horse and let him pull the wagon up off of your legs. Um, I need you to stand clear." The girl stands up and backs away from the wagon. She is still crying and sort of hiccupping. Ben feels really bad for her. He can't help but notice that she is beautiful. Even with her eyes and nose all red. These thoughts go through his head in the instant before he turns and scrambles back up the embankment. He unloads all of his stuff from Bens back and then he takes his rope and ties it across Ben's chest. He folds the blanket and puts it under the rope to cushion it. Ben backs up as close to the edge as he can and still have traction. Clyde climbs down the embankment and calls the girl over and hands her the rope and tells her to keep tension on it. She holds the rope while he looks for a place to tie it to the wagon. He decides to tie it to the axle but bring the rope up around the step. That will center the pull. He goes back over and takes the rope from the girl and she goes back over out of the way. He brings the rope around the step and ties it to the axle. He goes back over to the man and puts his arms under the man's arms and yells "Go Ben!" Ben pulls slowly and raises the wagon up off of the man. Clyde drags the man out from under the wagon. Ben slowly lowers the wagon back down and just stands there. Clyde checks out the man's legs and they look beat up but not broken. "You are very lucky sir." Clyde tells him. "It doesn't look like they're broken." The man says "I don't see how having a wagon lying on top of you for I know it must be three hours could be considered good luck young man." The girl with him giggles. He looks at her then. She has the bluest eyes he has ever seen. And they twinkle. He can see that she has blond curls poking out from under the edges of her hood, and dimples. His stomach flipflops. She looks to be about his age. He swallows hard and says "My name is Clyde Walton." The man grunts and shifts and reaches his hand out and says "My name is Charlie Parker and this is my daughter Elizabeth Parker." She says "Everyone calls me Betsy." Clyde blurts out, "I have a cow named Betsy, not calling you a cow, I mean, my family has a cow named Betsy. Um, I'm sorry, nice to meet you. Oh, uh, I'm Clyde." For some reason he can't talk to her. Not right anyway.

He turns back to the wagon. "I wonder if we can flip this back over." Mr. Parker says "It looks like there is some damage here. One of the wheels is broken." And Clyde says, "I guess your horses must have run off." Betsy looks around and says, "Fran and Speckle ran off when we flipped." Clyde just remembers that she was in the wreck too. "Are you alright?" He is looking at her worriedly. Her cape has opened up some and he can see that her dress is ripped on the sleeve and he can see a little blood there and there is a scratch on her hand. She has a bruise on her cheek. She says "I'm fine, just a little bumped and bruised." She looks around and says "Ooh, look there's Fran and Speckle." Clyde asks "Do you have a rope?" Mr. Parker is hobbling around looking at everything. About then he says "Here we go" and pulls out a rope. He unwinds it and pulls a knife out of a sheath hooked to his belt. He cuts the rope in half and hands half to Clyde and the other half to Betsy. She looks at him with that twinkle in her eye and says, "Let's go get'em amigo" and they start walking slowly in the direction of Fran and Speckle. It looks like they had settled down since the wreck. She goes in the direction of one of them and says, "Come on Franny, its okay now." She has already looped and tied her rope. Clyde doesn"t know when she did it. He quickly ties his and heads in the direction of the other horse. "Ok Speckle, let's do this." He eases closer to Speckle talking softly and he puts the rope over his head. He stays really calm. He looks over and sees that Betsy has Fran too. He pulls lightly on the rope and Speckle follows. They lead them back over to Mr. Parker and he checks them out and decides that they are ok.

"Well now what." They all sit on the ground and discuss what they should do. "Well, we can leave the wagon here and send someone back for it. I don't know if there will be anything left when we get back." Mr. Parker tells Clyde that he is moving himself and his daughter to Rapid City to run the land office. He tells him that he had been there before and had struck it rich. He has a working mine. His brother is taking care of the mine while he goes back to Sioux Falls to get his daughter and their things. "How far are we from Rapid City?" Clyde asks. "I figure we only have three days of travel left at the most, but that is with the wagon. On horseback we would make better time." Mr. Parker says. "I have a proposition for you Clyde. You look like an honest young man. What would you think if I offer to pay you to watch over my wagon until Betsy and I can make it to Rapid City and arrange for someone to come back and fetch our things? You can use anything you need to in the wagon and I will send the money back with my brother and his help." "How much are you talking about Mr. Parker?" "Let's say thirty dollars." That's a lot of money, Clyde thinks. That would get me started. He looks at Mr. Parker, sticks out his hand and says "It's a deal" and they shake.

Clyde climbs back up the embankment and loads all of his stuff back onto Ben. He tells Ben that he did an excellent job and pats him on the back. He goes back down the trail a little ways and finds a place to bring Ben down and they make their way back to the wagon. Meanwhile Mr. Parker and Betsy prepare their horses for the trip. Betsy says "I want to thank you for rescuing my father and for staying with the wagon. There are things that belonged to my Mama that I couldn't stand to lose. She passed when I was little. Thank you so much." Clyde just says "You two be safe." He is blushing bad and can't say anything else. Mr. Parker shakes his hand again and then Clyde helps Mr. Parker get up on his horse, he is pretty sore and Betsy gets up on hers without help and they leave.

Clyde looks around and says to Ben "I guess this is where we stay for a couple of days." All he sees in every direction is scrub land. It is starting to snow again. "Dang, I need shelter." He looks at the wagon. There is the canvas cover, but it is covering Mr. Parker's and Betsy's things. He walks to the back of the wagon and looks inside. He loosens the cover on the bottom side and stretches it out. He walks up the trail a ways and finds some hard sticks from the low bushes. He takes these back to the wagon wreck and stakes the canvas down. He crawls in. There isn't much room but it will work for the nights. He looks inside some more for blankets and finds two and a shawl. He looks at Ben. He is in a ditch so the cold wind is blocked on two sides. The wind is coming from the north. Good. He says to Ben, "Let's go have a look around." Clyde finds a little wooded area a short distance away and a creek. He takes Ben back to the wagon and leaves him there and goes back for an arm load of fire wood. He brings the wood back and goes back for supper. He walks around some more until he spots a rabbit. He shoots it and grabs another arm load of fire wood. He takes this back to the wagon. By this time it's evening. It had stopped snowing earlier and now it had started again. He unloads Ben and puts a blanket over his back. He puts his wolf hide over his on shoulders and builds a fire. He cooks his rabbit over the fire, puts another blanket over Ben and crawls inside his makeshift shelter. He hunkers inside and eats his rabbit. When he is done he takes the bones away from his camp and then comes back and lay down for the night. Later on he wakes up with Ben's head inside the wagon cover. He had kneeled down and stuck his head in. Clyde couldn't believe it, he went back to sleep with a smile on his face.

The next morning the ground is covered with snow. It isn't deep, just a few inches. Ben had gotten up off of the ground and was standing. Clyde figured the ground probably got cold. He built a fire as quickly as he could, found some coffee inside the wagon and had a cup. That day he just stays close to the wagon, he explores the countryside around it some and then takes a nap. He goes hunting in the little wooded area and shoots a rabbit. He hadn't spent such a leisure day in a long time. It was cold but it hadn't snowed again. That evening he builds a good warm fire and cooks his rabbit. After he's done eating, he covers Ben up good and crawls into the wagon. He lays there thinking about Betsy. She sure is pretty. He thinks about her twinkling blue eyes and dimples and about seeing her again. If Ben had joined him inside his cover again during the night Clyde slept through it. The next day went about the same way except it had snowed more. The ground is covered pretty well now. Clyde wears every piece of clothing he owns and he keeps his wolf hide wrapped around him all day. He thinks about Betsy a lot and he is anxious to move on. He spends five days there.

Early evening on the fifth day he notices a wagon coming down the trail. There are a couple of men in front. They look like miners. When they come up Clyde raises his rifle and has it pointed at them. There are three of them in all. The driver says "Howdy, I'm Joel Parker, Charlie's brother, you must be Clyde." Clyde lowers his rifle as the two men in front climb down. The one that is sitting next to the driver looks to be about Clyde's age. This is my son Harold, we call him Harry. Another man climbs down from the back. This is Toby. He works with us. They all shake hands. Clyde has gathered his stuff together earlier hoping that today would be the day that he could move on. They all work together to load all of the Parkers things onto the empty wagon. They were done in a couple of hours and Joel Parker paid Clyde his thirty dollars. They spent the night there and left the next morning.

They were all headed the same way when they left so they traveled together toward Rapid City. It felt good to have company. Each evening they would sit around the campfire and talk. Harry would play his mouth harp and Joel would sing. They would all laugh and joke. Clyde had a great time. Ben didn't have an episode. He really can't think of anything else to call it. He is sad when they arrive in Rapid City three days later. He is also excited to see Betsy again. When they arrive they all go to the Parkers house. Their house is huge and beautiful. There is a big porch that wraps around the whole front. There is a bench swing and rocking chairs. A butler answers the door and they find Mr. Parker sitting in the parlor when they arrive. He has healed some since he had last seen him. He shakes his hand and Mr. Parker slaps him on the back so hard that he thinks he might fall over. They visit for a while and Clyde finally gets up the courage to ask about Betsy. Mr. Parker says "She's at the church at some ladies group or something." "She should be home anytime." Clyde tries to pay attention to the conversation until he hears the front door open and Betsy comes into the parlor. She is more beautiful than he remembers even. She is wearing a dark blue cape with fur around the edge of the hood and a blue dress and matching bonnet that make her eyes seem even bluer. When she sees him she smiles and there is that twinkle. He is in love. He can hardly talk, but he manages a "Hello again, Ms. Parker." That's all he has to say because after that she takes over. "Well, Mr. Clyde Walton, how do you do?" She held out her small gloved hand and he grabbed it and shook it like he would shake a man's hand. He's wondering what happens to him when she's around and turns bright red again. Her teeth probably knocked together with that handshake. She just giggles and says, "My goodness, now that's a hand shake." They talk for a minute, or she does, all he can do is stand there. She tells him that they are planning a winter dance in a week and that he should come. All he can do is nod his head yes. She says, "That would be great, we can go together, since you're new here and all." and she giggles again. She tells him when the dance is and that he can pick her up at six o'clock. "I need to go in and change, good bye for now Mr. Walton." All he can do is nod. He looks over at Mr. Parker and sees that he is smiling. It looks like he is trying to keep from laughing. Not long after that he bids his farewell to Mr. Parker, Joel, Harry, and Toby. He's anxious to see the Black Hills and he needs to find a place to camp before nightfall.

They head out of town to the southwest toward the Black Hills. When they get a couple of miles out of town it starts snowing. Clyde takes his wolf hide loose from his saddle and wraps it around himself. The snow starts coming down harder and he thinks about turning around and going back to town. He notices that Ben is acting funny again. He wants to move faster toward the hills. He snorts and speeds up as the snow falls harder. Clyde says "Ben please, not now." He keeps going and all that Clyde can do is hold on for dear life. They go like this for what seems like at least an hour. Clyde can't see a foot in front of his face. The wind is blowing so hard he has his arms wrapped around Ben's neck and he is holding on with his legs too. He feels briars grabbing his arms and legs as they go into brush. They stop. The wind doesn't feel as strong here. He realizes his eyes are closed and opens them. It looks like they are in a bush next to a hill. There is a little clearing here. The ground is sandy and there is a place on the rock hillside that looks like a small cave. The brush is so thick here that it is blocking the wind. He can hear the wind blowing outside of this space though. He climbs down and turns in a circle and says "Where have you brought me?" "Why?" He is looking at Ben and sees that sad look that he had seen before. He walks over to where the opening in the side of the hill is and looks in. It is about four foot by four foot. It's dark and he can't see anything. "I hope you didn't bring me to rescue a bear."

He finds a stick and tears a long strip off of one of the blankets. He wraps this around the end of the stick and makes a torch. He gathers up some limbs and dead wood he finds in this little hiding place and builds a fire. He lights the torch, grabs his rifle and goes into the cave. He just goes a little ways in when he sees the gold in the walls. He sees a rock on the floor of the cave and he picks it up and scratches around on the wall. It's real. He can't breathe. "Oh my God, oh thank you, my God" Ooooh" He's feels dizzy and has to sit down. And he cries. It all hasn't been for nothing. He can bring his family here. He can see his family again. He runs out of the cave yelling "WooHooo!" "Oh Ben, my Ben, You did it!" "I can see Mama, and Joseph and Luke and Rose and Emily again, My Family!" He throws his arms around Ben and hugs him.

He unpacks his tools and he puts them in the cave. He takes his whittling knife and digs out a couple of nuggets. He pulls a long inch wide strip off of his blanket and a square piece. He puts the nuggets in the center of the square, brings the corners up and ties the string around it. He peeks out of the brush where they are hidden. It is still snowing hard and the wind is blowing. It is a full blown snow storm. So Clyde starts working his mine using his Pa's whittling knife. He digs out a few more nuggets and adds them to the ones he already has. He figures when he gets to town he will go talk to Mr. Parker. He will ask him what to do now. He feels like he can trust him and he doesn't want anyone to know about his find until he has it legally claimed. He is so wound up that day and there is no one to tell his news to. The weather is too bad for him to hunt for his food, but he has some beans left. He melts some snow and cooks beans for his supper. That night he sits beside his fire and talks to Ben. He tells him how he is going to buy a wagon and another mule, so he can go get Jack. He will buy a good wagon so he can go get his family. It is early yet, but he decides he is going to marry Betsy. That night he can hardly sleep. Sleep finely comes in the early morning hours.

He wakes up early even though he doesn't get much sleep. He had slept in the cave wrapped in his hide and he had covered Ben with the two blankets he had. Ben seems really cold. He decides he needs to leave so they both can move around and warm up and he is anxious to talk to Mr. Parker and Betsy. It has stopped snowing and the wind has died down. Clyde leaves all of his stuff in the cave except for the nuggets. He tries to cover his tracks as best as he can. The place is very hidden. He wouldn't have ever found it if it weren't for Ben. He isn't sure which direction they had come because Ben had brought them here. He just climbs on Ben's back and lets him lead them back to town. He uses the knife to mark trees and watches for landmarks so he can tell Mr. Parker where it is located so he can help him claim it.

When he reaches town everything is crazy just like in Sioux Falls. People are everywhere and it is loud. He is a little more prepared this time. He does just like the black smith in Tulsa told him. He tries to not draw any attention to himself. He rides Ben through town looking around. He can't really see his family living here but the Parkers seemed to do ok. He sees a sign that reads "Rapid City Land Office" and heads in that direction. He ties Ben to the hitching post outside and goes in. As soon as he gets inside the door he spots Mr. Parker. He is standing over a map on his counter talking to a customer. He glances up and smiles and raises his index finger indicating it would take him a minute. Clyde wonders over to a wall that has all kinds of advertisements on it. He sees one for a wagon and mule for sale for thirty dollars. He also sees a lot of advertisements for men looking for work. He can hear Mr. Parker and the man discuss a couple of plots. After about ten minutes of discussion the man decides which one he wants of the two he is thinking about. Mr. Parker writes a paper out and they both sign it. They shake hands and the man leaves.

Mr. Parker turns to Clyde as soon as the man leaves and says "Clyde my boy, how are you doing today?" "Good morning Mr. Parker. I'm fine." "I need to talk to you in private, it's important." Mr. Parker says, "We're alone now, Clyde."Clyde looks at him nervously and says, "Can we lock the door for a minute?" Mr. Parker shakes his head slowly and says "ok" and walks over and locks the door. "Mr. Parker I feel like I can trust you. You seem like an honorable man. I need help. You're the only person I know to ask." Clyde looks so distressed that Mr. Parker says, "It's ok Clyde, you can trust me, what's wrong?" "Well, I struck gold and I don't know what to do now?" All that Mr. Parker can say is, "How? You just got here. What do you mean?" Clyde didn't think he could tell him about Ben without him thinking he was crazy so he told him that he was riding out and it started to snow and before he knew it he was in a snow storm. He said he accidently found this cave and when he looked inside there was gold in the walls. Mr. Parker just laughed and laughed. Clyde was saying "I'm serious Mr. Parker, there's gold, bunches of it." Mr. Parker got serious then. "First you have to stake your claim." Come over here." He heads over to the map on the counter. "Show me where." Clyde looks at him. He looks into his eyes, searching. Mr. Parker says, "You can trust me, Clyde" He sees in his eyes that he can. He looks at the map and Mr. Parker explains it some so he can pin point where the cave is. When he shows him, he says, "Humph, I would never have guessed. No one has even been digging in that area." He says, "Alright let's make it yours." He writes up the papers and gets Clyde to sign and then he signs as a witness. He shakes his hand and says "Congratulations, Clyde. No one deserves it more than you." "Come to dinner tonight, we need to celebrate." Clyde agrees. Where do I cash this in and he pulls out his piece of blanket with the gold in it and opens it up. Mr. Parker, eyes wide, says, "Oh my." He takes a piece out to look at closer. He pulls a monacle out of his pocket, put it to his eye and looks closely at it. "You can just spend it like currency." "I will lend you one of my men for protection." "Clyde says, "Do you really think that's necessary?" "Yeah, I do young man. You may be rich now." Clyde tells him that he needs to go gather supplies he will need to start up. Mr. Parker tells Clyde that he will go with him to help him find what he needs. He grabs his coat, hat and scarf. He flips the open sign over and tells Clyde, "We can go by my house on the way out to your claim so I can let our housekeeper know that I am leaving for a bit." We can pick up a couple of my hands there to go with us."

He ends up buying the wagon and mule that is advertised on the board in the land office. The mule is a jenny. Ben and one of Mr. Parker's horses pull the wagon with the jenny tied to the back. Ben seems calm through all of this. They go from there to the Parkers house. When they get there Clyde stays outside while Mr. Parker goes in. He can hear him yelling "Izzy, where are you?" He comes back out in a short time. He has a bag with food in it and he hands it to Clyde as he climbs back up on the wagon and asks Clyde to pull around the house and follow a little dirt track about fifty yards to the horse barns. There is a big grizzly looking man sitting on a stump oiling a saddle and another smaller man standing beside him. They are discussing the right way to oil leather. Mr. Parker introduces them as Jonas and Sam. Clyde can tell that they have known each other for years by the way they talk. They shake hands and Mr. Parker asks if they would mind riding with them. It is decided that Jonas will be Clyde's protection. Clyde agrees to pay him three dollars a week. It would only be until Clyde can find his own help. They all load up and head to Clyde's claim.

As they leave Mr. Parker hands the bag with food in it to Clyde and tells him, "Eat." Clyde is starving so he wastes no time pulling a chicken leg out of the bag and eating it as they leave. It takes about three hours to get there. Clyde is glad that he had marked the way. When he says, "Here we are!" all of the others are looking around wondering where it is. The brush in front of the cave has it hidden so well that none of them can see it. He climbs down, ties Jenny to the brush and takes a lantern from the back of the wagon. It already has oil in it. He separates some branches and disappears from sight. The others do the same and they find themselves in a very small clearing with the cave on the opposite side. He lights the lantern and they go in. It is really small so Jonas won't even fit. He and Sam both stay outside. They shine the lantern around and the walls have little areas here and there where the gold is visible. Mr. Parker's jaw has dropped. He says, "It's a rich one my boy, my god look at this." Clyde is just beaming. His face hurts from smiling so big. He starts telling Mr. Parker about how he wants to go get his family and move them here. He has seen a nice spot not far from the mine to build a house. He noticed it on the way. He figures his brother can help him. He will be sixteen soon. He says, "That sounds grand my young friend." "I'll do whatever I can to help." They stake the mine and head back to Mr. Parkers house. Jonas and Sam stay at the mine with Jenny and the wagon and supplies. Clyde and Mr. Parker ride their horses back.

They had a grand celebration that evening. Mr. Parker's brother Joel and his family were there. Mr. Parker and Clyde talked a lot about what needed to be done at the mine. He talked to his brother about covering the land office for a while so he can help Clyde get started. He was able see Betsy again. She was dressed in a beautiful blue velvet gown. Her hair was up, but she had springy curls sticking out all over and those

117

twinkling eyes. His heart felt like it skipped a beat when he saw her. Sometimes they sat and talked. He wasn't quite as tongue tied as the other times. He stayed in the guest room that night and the next morning they started early. They worked hard the next month but he had a working mine by the end of it. Ben had been very calm. No agitation. He seemed a little sad though.

In the next month they built a nice big house. Betsy would ride up and bring food. Sometime they sat and talked. All of Clyde's dreams were coming true. On the night before he was going to set out for Oklahoma he lay in his new bed in his new house and thought about his family. He was so excited that it took him awhile to get to sleep. When he did, he dreamed. In the dream he saw his father as he had been before he had gotten sick. He was sitting on their old porch whittling and Clyde was sitting beside him. His father tells him, "The eyes see clearer when the heart is open. Remember this. I must leave you now. You are a man. Take care of our family. I will miss you." While he was looking at his father, his father's head kept changing into a horse head and then back into his own head. It was Ben. He was seeing his father turning into Ben and then back into himself again. He could see that sad look in his eyes. "I love you forever." Clyde woke up crying and climbed out of bed wondering. He went out to the barn to check on Ben. When he reached the barn he picked up the lantern by the door and lit it. He went in slowly. He was feeling dread and didn't know why. It was just a dream, wasn't it? When he reached Ben's stall he was gone. Just like he had appeared now he had disappeared and Clyde mourned his father.

THE END

Sunflowers and Moonbeams

"I'll bring the butterfly wings and nut butter dip."

She is called Sunflower and he is called Moonbeam. Sunflower has long hair and wears a peasant blouse and a skirt. She has flowers in her hair. Moonbeam wears faded jeans, with holes in the knees and a t-shirt. He has long hair too and wears a bandana tied around his head. They just float through life spreading peace and love. They live in a van and drive around and entertain people on the sidewalks of the city. Moonbeam plays his guitar and Sunflower sings and plays her tambourine. She has a soothing hypnotic voice. People always stop and get lost in her song. Everyone always sees them as different, they are dressed from another era, but nobody really knows just how different they are.

There is also a priest that works at the homeless shelter and soup kitchen at the Catholic Church. He is called Father John. He is thirty years old with red hair and freckles. There is Ruby and Joe. Ruby is a mousey little woman with dark hair and eyes. She's a first grade teacher. Joe is a carpenter. A big teddy bear. Then there is Fred and Alice. They are an older couple in their seventies. They are actually from another planet. Their planet is called Bindle. On Bindle they have no war, hunger or crime. Everyone is happy and content. They are on a mission here. They are trying to teach humans how to love each other again.

Fred and Alice live in a small apartment. All of the Bindle missionaries meet at their apartment once a week. There are others around this city and elsewhere around the world. This is just one sector. They discuss ways to get humans to care again.

Alice and Fred are sitting in their living room. They are a couple even on Bindle. "You know Fred I'm running out of ideas." "Me too honey." They have adapted their language to earth, after doing research they discovered this is how humans from earth communicate. They usually just think what they want to say. They have a few other abilities too. They also had to alter the way they look. They both have gray hair and wrinkles. Don't know what happened to Sunflower and Moonbeam, they were different on Bindle too. "I think it is time for us to do something drastic. Nothing has worked so far." "Your right Alice, I agree, but what? Let's bring this up at the meeting tonight. Maybe the others will have some ideas." "Are you hungry, we have some fresh crickets in the fridge?" "Thanks sweetie that sounds good. Are there anymore of those bean sprouts and minnows?" "Yeah, I'll get us some of those too and some honey water."

That evening they all begin to arrive. First Sunflower and Moonbeam, then about ten minutes later Father John. Then Ruby and Joe. They all greet each other in the Bindle way. They bow slightly to either side while making a clicking sound. Fred always starts the meeting. "Hello everyone, so nice to see you. Please make yourselves comfortable." Everyone finds a place to sit and the meeting begins. "Alice and I were talking and we feel that it is time for us to do something drastic. We can show love and kindness until we are blue in the face, oh yeah that's how we usually look." He chuckles, "I'm sorry; I just get so tired of pretending to be human. Anyway I thought I would bring this up to you and see what kind of ideas we can come up with. We need to do something that will make the humans care again. Does anyone have any ideas?" Everyone was quiet, as if in thought. Ruby says, "How about if we reward them for being nice like I do with my students? "That's an idea." Fred replies, 'But what if they just be nice for the reward, that's not going to last."

"Any more ideas?" Fred asks. Joe answers "If we could get the humans to work together towards some goal. Maybe that would draw them together." The others were shaking their heads and saying, "Yeah, that might work." But what kind of goal?" Alice asks. 'Survival tends to draw humans together." Moonbeam replies. "If everyone was on the same level, somehow." says Sunflower. "Let's all just think about it and we'll discuss it again next week. Now on to our other issues." They discussed different topics for a while and then everyone went their separate ways.

When they leave Sunflower and Moonbeam go out and get into their van. They are a couple on Bindle too. They drive down to the beach and open the back doors of the van. They have a mattress in the back so they just lay on it and listen to the ocean. Sunflower says, "What do you think?" "I don't know. I don't understand why they don't want to love each other just because it feels right." "Maybe if the humans had to depend on each other more they would learn. Like if half of them had no arms and the other half had no legs or something like that." Sunflower sits up and so does Moonbeam. She asks, "What if half couldn't see and half couldn't hear. They would have to help each other." "Maybe, it might work. We'll bring it up at the next meeting."

The next week they all met at Fred and Alice's apartment. The meeting started as usual. Everybody had been thinking on the problem. Sunflower and Moonbeam told them about the idea they had about half with no hearing and half with no sight. They all talked about it and decided to take it to the head of the Bindle missionaries. "We'll find out what they think and discuss it again next week." They went on to other topics and then everyone went their separate ways.

Sunflower and Moonbeam did their usual things all week. They watched the humans even closer than usual and envisioned them helping each other. They were thinking of situations like a young deaf gangster helping a blind business man find a cab. Or a deaf Muslim man helping a scantily clad blind woman find an address. Humans with completely different beliefs helping each other instead of fighting. They were getting more excited about the idea all of the time.

Meanwhile, the others were doing the same thing. They were all thinking about how everyone would help each other and live happily ever after. Fred and Alice were thinking about the elderly at the senior center helping the nurses and aids and helping each other instead of bickering. The priest was envisioning the homeless ones helping each other. The drug addicts helping the alcoholics and mentally ill. Joe was thinking about the construction workers helping each other. The ones that can see would cut the boards and the ones that can't see would hold it for them or help in other ways. Everyone helping each other. Ruby is imagining all the parents helping each other with their kids. All working together to help them grow up to become good adults.

Fred and Alice had communicated with their head missionaries and they had talked to the leaders on their planet and they agreed to give it a try. They had been working on this situation for a long time and nothing had worked. The scientists on Bindle are ahead of the ones on earth, probably due to their ability to work together so well. They don't have the ambition and jealousy they have on earth. They communicate better for that reason. Their scientist on Bindle created a spray that reacts to the pigment in eye color. More pigment would cause a reaction, loss of sight and the ears would swell shut for about two hours. Less pigment would not react. It takes very little to work. They would have a whole fleet of ships fly all around earth and spray this, it will take about an hour and everyone with brown or darker eyes would lose their sight. They would also lose their hearing for about two hours. The scientist then created a supersonic sound that would cause deafness in the humans that didn't' react to the spray. These same ships would wait about an hour after the spray to make sure everyone has reacted and then they would make the sound. It is so loud that it would affect people all over the world. So everyone with blue, green or hazel eyes would become deaf. Everything was set in motion.

At the next meeting Fred and Alice were able to update everybody, "It's going to happen". When they all get together, everybody is excited. They all laugh and talk about how great it is going to be. The event would happen in two weeks. They decided to meet at Fred and Alice's apartment on the date of the great change. That's what they started calling it "The Great Change". Sunflower said, "You know when the great change happens we are going to have to go out and help people adjust." "Yeah, and we'll also need to close our ears when the big sound comes, it won't make us deaf but it is pretty loud, it might hurt our ears if we leave them open." says Fred. "They said we are safe from the spray, being different and all." "Sunflower and I will bring some dried beetles and coconut milk for the great change." says Moonbeam. "I'll bring some fresh grubs." says Father John. "I'll bring some butterfly wings and nut butter dip" says Joe. "I'll bring the sugar water." Ruby adds. "Alice and I will put a table up on the roof and everybody can bring chairs. Bring your scope helmets if you want, we just can't get caught wearing them."

They did their usual things with an underlying excitement. Their next meeting they made plans on how they would handle the great change. They discussed how they would have to help calm everyone. They decided to load their finger pins with sedative in case people panic and they could use Sunflowers hypnotic song to calm the blind, once they get their hearing back that is. And Moonbeam could make beautiful colors that could calm the deaf. Ruby could help the kids and Joe would be muscle and hugs. Father John would help people find peace. Fred and Alice have that wise old grandma and grandpa calming effect on people. All of the other missionaries on earth were preparing too.

The big day arrived. 'The Great Change' was scheduled to start at nine o'clock on Saturday, that is when the cause and effects came together. Everybody started arriving at Fred and Alice's at seven. Joe, Moonbeam and Fred started moving the table and stuff up to the roof. They all had their scope helmets in bags and they brought chairs and snacks. They put all the food out on the table and moved their chairs to the edge of the roof so they would have a good view. They knew they would have to go down and help. They figured they would just fly down, with everything going on, no one would notice. They all sat down and excitedly waited. Moonbeam said, "What time is it?" "It is eight fifty five." says Fred. They put on their helmet scopes. They sat in anticipation and then they felt a slight hot breeze out of nowhere and knew. They were spraying.

They all looked over the edge of the building and saw the people on the sidewalks; a lot of them just stopped and put their arms out in front of them. Some of them were running into each other, fire hydrants, signs, parked cars. Cars and trucks were crashing into each other, parked cars and running up onto the sidewalks and into pedestrians. Everyone was screaming and yelling for help. There were some that weren't affected and they were helping the ones that couldn't see or hear. They were pulling them out of in front of cars and trucks. All of the missionaries on the roof stood up, looked at each other, removed their helmets and jumped over the edge of the roof. They just swooped down and nobody noticed with everything else going on. They began calming people down as best as they could. They all know they have one hour until they shut their ears. They communicated without speaking, that it is time. They closed their ears.

The ones that kept their sight all of a sudden have strange looks on their faces. They put their hands up to their ears and they are screaming and yelling I can't hear and help! They all have pleading looks on their faces. The missionaries know that it is over so they open their ears up. The ones that were helping the blind had stopped. The missionaries start helping them too. Moonbeam plays his guitar and beautiful colors flowed from his fingers as he plays. Everyone that sees the colors sighs and relaxes. All of the missionaries are sedating people and letting everyone know that it is going to be ok. After a while Sunflower starts to sing. It takes awhile for everyone to calm down.

And for about a year it looked like things would be like they thought. People were working together to do things. They were caring about each other. Then groups started to form. It started because the ones with the same color eyes were from the same places. African Americans, Hispanics, Asians mostly have darker eyes and English, Irish and Germans mostly have lighter eyes. People were still different. People were still fighting. This just added another difference.

The End

About the Author

I am southern born and raised. When I began writing this book I lived on a chicken farm in Pollock, Louisiana with my best friend, my puppy dog, and chickens everywhere. Since then I have moved to Red Oak, Iowa.